low
red
moon

low
red
moon

Ivy Devlin

BLOOMSBURY

NEW YORK BERLIN LONDON

First published in the United States of America in September 2010
by Bloomsbury Books for Young Readers
www.bloomsburyteens.com

For information about permission to reproduce selections from this book, write to
Permissions, Bloomsbury BFYR, 175 Fifth Avenue, New York, New York 10010

Library of Congress Cataloging-in-Publication Data
Devlin, Ivy.
Low red moon / by Ivy Devlin.—1st U.S. ed.
p.   cm.
Summary: Seventeen-year-old Avery can remember nothing to explain her
parents' violent death in the woods where they live, but after meeting Ben, a
mysterious new neighbor, she begins to believe some of the stories she has
heard about creatures of the forest.
ISBN 978-1-59990-510-5 (hc)
[1. Forests—Fiction.   2. Wolves—Fiction.   3. Shapeshifting—Fiction.
4. Murder—Fiction.   5. Interpersonal relations—Fiction.
6. Grandmothers—Fiction.]   I. Title.
PZ7.D49842Lo 2010   [Fic]—dc22   2010003480
ISBN 978-1-59990-618-8 (pb)

Book design by Danielle Delaney
Typeset by Westchester Book Composition
Printed in the U.S.A. by Worldcolor Fairfield, Pennsylvania
2 4 6 8 10 9 7 5 3 1 (hc)
2 4 6 8 10 9 7 5 3 1 (pb)

low
red
moon

one

I was covered in blood when the police found me.

Head to toe: in my hair, on my eyelashes, in the skin between my toes. Dried so deep into my clothes they were taken away and I never saw them again.

I found flecks of it under my fingernails for days after, dried reddish brown crumbs that I clung to as they fell free, that I held as if I could somehow pull them inside me.

As if I could somehow bring my parents back.

I didn't remember what happened to them. I didn't remember finding them. I didn't remember sitting down with their ... with their bodies. I didn't remember sitting with them as the night-gleaming moon rose, arching across the sky, and the stars shone.

I was with them all night in the forest. I didn't remember that either.

I didn't even remember being found. Ron said he'd found me after he'd gotten a call from Deputy Sharpe, who was out patrolling the little section of forest where people lived. Ron had come to find the deputy crying, and me . . .

And me.

I was just sitting there, but when I was in the hospital I heard him tell Renee that at first he'd thought I was dead too. That I wasn't moving. Wasn't blinking.

That I was sitting on the ground outside my home covered in blood.

That I was sitting with my parents' bodies, holding their hands in mine.

That I'd tried to put what was left of them back together. That all the blood on me came from me trying to make them whole when they were broken. From me trying to put them back together.

I couldn't do it.

My parents were dead.

They'd died and no one knew how or why, just that it had happened.

They hadn't just died, though.

My parents were murdered.

Ron was sure I'd seen something. Heard something. I was in the hospital for two days after they found me; not because I was hurt, but because I wouldn't move. I wouldn't talk, wouldn't eat, and wouldn't speak. Everything inside me was dark. Gone.

It was like I was dead too, just like Ron had thought when he'd first seen me.

But I wasn't dead, and Renee made me leave the hospital for the funeral. She stood next to me, holding my hand while the wooden boxes that held my parents were put in the ground. The boxes were closed tight, but I didn't wonder if my parents were in there. I knew they were gone forever.

I knew that because the one thing I did remember is what I saw when Ron put me in his car. Deputy Sharpe was off sobbing softly in the distance, the sound coming to me like it was the wind. Like noise, and nothing more.

I remembered looking out Ron's window and hearing the crying. I remembered seeing the colors of sirens cast shadows everywhere. I didn't hear the sirens, though. In the car, I didn't hear anything but silence.

I watched those colored shadows on the ground and I watched them flicker off pieces of plastic sheeting. I remembered it looked strange to see them there, covering the soil and snaking around the trees my parents loved.

I remembered the lumps under it.

I remembered screaming then, screaming until my voice stopped.

So when I saw the boxes, I knew who was in them.

I knew my parents were gone.

I watched them being lowered into the ground, I saw soil start to cover them up, and I stared at the trees

Renee pressed into the dirt, tiny saplings that would one day grow tall and true. That would grow into trees like those in the forest.

I heard her whisper, *"Why, John? Why?"* her voice angry and sad but mostly angry, so angry, as she did it, and then watched her stand up, brushing the soil off her hands. It fell free easily, smoothly.

I closed my eyes and saw dark red.

I saw blood.

And around that, through that, I saw silver, gleaming silver, a blur of something cruel. Inhuman.

"Avery?" Renee said, and I opened my eyes. Saw the soil where my parents would forever lie.

I didn't remember finding them. I didn't even remember the last thing I said to them. It was all gone.

And yet I was still here.

two

I went to school the day after the funeral. Renee said I didn't have to go, but I didn't know what else to do. I wasn't allowed to go home. I had a few things from there, brought over in boxes, but that was it. The house was still a crime scene and Ron wouldn't let me go out there at all.

"But you're the sheriff," I'd said to him in the hospital, as he and I sat waiting for Renee to sign the paperwork to check me out. He sighed.

"I know," he said. "But you can't go out there. Not now. Not yet."

"When?" I said, but he shook his head, no answer at all.

So my choices were to sit in Renee's house, spending the day with a grandmother I didn't know, or go to school.

I knew the people there better than I knew her, and I kept thinking about what she'd said at the funeral. How there'd been so much anger in what she'd whispered to my father.

School was easier to deal with.

It shouldn't have been. There should have been stares and whispers, and maybe there were and I didn't notice them. I was just glad to be out of Renee's house, out of the reminder that her blue guest room was my room now.

That my house—my parents, my world—was gone.

I sat through my first three classes just like always, in the back watching everyone else. My father hadn't liked the schools in Woodlake—he'd been through them and thought they taught "crap." He'd been so sure he hadn't learned enough that the summer before he started college in Chicago he took the bus there and spent all his time reading everything he could in the public library.

"I had so much to learn," he always said, "and I don't want that for you," so I spent fifteen years learning at the kitchen table with Mom and not going to Woodlake schools.

Mom was a good teacher. The ones at the high school were okay, but they didn't come up with anything like Mom did. In English, we were reading *Julius Caesar*, but I'd already read some of Shakespeare's plays when I was thirteen, and then watched movies of them and wrote

about how the themes were so universal they could be filmed over and over again.

I knew the play, and so I was ready to talk about it, but the discussion wasn't anything like the one Mom and I would have had. All the teacher talked about was Brutus and what he did. Why he did it.

No one wondered about Julius. About his drive. His will. Why he made the choices he made.

Mom had made me think about it.

She would have asked me about it; she liked hearing about school and had been the one to talk Dad into letting me go in the first place. He'd only agreed because Mom's business—she made and sold wild fruit preserves, and some singer swore in a magazine article that a diet of them and rice crackers kept her thin—had taken off and we'd needed the money she was able to make.

The paper Dad worked for, *The Woodlake Daily*, kept cutting staff, kept cutting salaries, and really only survived because the owner was old and believed everyone should start the day reading the paper, even if she had to basically give it away.

I had been excited about going to high school when I started last year. I loved my parents, but I wanted to make friends. Meet guys. I'd seen some cute ones around town, and I wanted to talk to them. I wanted them to want to talk to me. I wanted to be like the people who lived in town.

I didn't want to be like me and my parents were; I didn't want my whole life to be the forest. I didn't want to be like the Thantos family, who lived in the woods just like we did, but who hardly ever went into town and who always looked vaguely startled when they did, as if the small cluster of buildings that made up Woodlake's main street was enormous, overwhelming.

I didn't want to be like their daughter, Jane, who I'd only met a handful of times, and who could talk for hours about the forest but who didn't want to watch TV or even talk about books, who said, "I don't know who that is," whenever I'd asked her about someone I'd seen in town.

But high school wasn't—it wasn't hard, but it wasn't easy either. The guys I'd seen in town, the ones who were so cute, weren't so cute in school. They looked all right, but they didn't talk about anything real. They just laughed at dumb things or talked about what movie or person or TV show sucked most.

I knew that was normal, I did. But I had pictured guys who did more than check out my chest when they looked at me. I wanted more than guys who frowned over the lack of my chest and then said stuff like, "So you got taught by your mom, huh? That must have sucked."

The girls were even harder. They just ignored me. They'd known each other since I was five and learning my ABCs in the kitchen with Mom while they went to

Woodlake Elementary. They'd been through birthday parties and slumber parties, boyfriend problems and shopping trips to the nearest mall, two hours away.

They knew who I was, but I wasn't part of their world, and with graduation not in the distant future but close—an almost they could taste—they didn't need me. They had each other, and the one girl I did become friends with only talked to me because no one else talked to her.

Kirsta had been popular, but that was back in middle school and long forgotten by everyone but her. She held on to that time tightly, though, pulled it out and unfolded it for me to hear. She told me about the birthday parties girls who now looked through her used to beg to attend. How she used to have a different boyfriend every week when all the guys did was sneer at her now.

Kirsta had been a star, but in fifth grade her mother died and her dad married his secretary three months later. Even I'd heard about that, and in Woodlake being different—or doing something different—wasn't a good thing.

So when I started high school, Kirsta was different too, wasn't a star at all. In fact, she was so far down the social ladder that she was willing to talk to me. She and I only saw each other at school, though. We didn't have a real friendship, but it was the closest thing to one I'd ever had, even if I knew she only talked to me because I'd listen to her stories about the way her life used to be.

And on the day I came to school from Renee's house and not my own, I knew that our "friendship" was over as soon as I passed her in the hall before lunch.

I knew because I saw her see me, and watched her turn away.

I could understand why she did it. Before, I'd been Avery Hood, the quiet girl who lived in the woods like a few other people did. But now I was Avery Hood, the girl whose parents had been murdered, the girl who'd been found with their bodies. Kirsta had lost her mother, but not like I had.

I was the girl who'd been found with her parents' bodies. I was the girl who couldn't remember what had happened. Who should have had a story to tell but didn't.

I was the girl who'd been covered in blood but who hadn't had a mark on her.

So I ate lunch by myself, picking at the chicken nuggets on my cafeteria tray. Mom always made lunch for me before, and it was strange not to be eating a sandwich on her homemade bread. I'd hated it, actually—the heavy weight of it and how it didn't even look like regular bread—but now I missed it. I missed everything about Mom and Dad.

"She never even really talked about her parents," I heard Kirsta say, and looked over to where we used to sit, saw her grinning as girls she used to rule years ago stood looking at her, smiling to show they were being kind.

That they were letting her in, even if it was only for a little while.

"I mean, she *never* talked about them, like maybe she ... you know ... ," Kirsta said, drawing out the last words to let silence and speculation reign, and I pushed my tray away and got up.

It was true; I hadn't talked about my parents. I hadn't needed to. I was happy with them, and Kirsta had her own stories to tell, a never-ending supply of them, all once-upon-a-time stories that ended with her father bringing home someone to replace her mother, and how people had stared and talked and then forgotten her.

I wanted to hate her for what she'd said, but I watched her smile at the girls clustered around her, saw how happy she was to be seen again, and knew it was what she'd always wanted. And I couldn't get upset over that. It just seemed wrong to waste tears over her. To cry over something as small as a story when what was true and real for me—what had been my life—was gone.

Still, my eyes stung anyway.

I left the cafeteria and somehow kept going, even though school dragged on and on and on. I trudged to my last class, Art, wearily.

I'd signed up for it because Kirsta had, and because Mom and I had always drawn together at home. I wasn't any good, but it hadn't mattered to Mom. I'd learned about technique and looked at famous paintings, and

we'd talked about what made them beautiful. Mom said that loving art was just as important as being able to create it.

Here, loving art didn't matter, and I walked in to see the same bowl of apples that had been defeating me since—and it was strange to have to think this way, to have to think of before and now and my parents in that way.

But I did, and that bowl of apples had been defeating me since before my parents died. They were shiny, perfect-looking, plastic.

Fake.

Kirsta was working on the other side of the room, away from her usual spot near me. I stood alone and looked at those unchanging apples and the drawing I'd started. I'd wanted to make the apples look like they should after they'd been in a bowl for a few days. I'd made the skin spotted, shown rot creeping in.

I thought it would be realistic to show how things were. To show that things die.

But that was before.

I closed my sketchpad and asked to go to the bathroom. I went to the front office instead and asked them to call Renee.

"Renee? You mean your grandmother, Avery?" Mrs. Jones, the school's secretary, said, and I nodded. She knew that my parents didn't talk to my grandmother.

Everyone did. And she clearly had chosen a side. Everyone else had too, back when my parents stopped talking to Renee, and most sided with her because they found my parents a little strange, a little "off."

I swallowed. I wanted to tell her that she didn't know my parents like I did, that she didn't know anything, but just sat down to wait instead. She wouldn't listen to anything I said anyway.

As I settled onto the uncomfortable office sofa, someone rushed in, the door flying open, and I got a glimpse of a guy. Dark hair, an old, soft-looking T-shirt, and jeans and moccasins.

No guy at school wore moccasins. Someone new?

I leaned forward a bit, to get a better look, and then—of course—the guy turned and caught me looking at him.

His eyes met mine for a second, and I realized he'd never look at me. Never really look, anyway. His face made every other guy's pale into nothing. It was all stark angles: cheekbones, mouth, and a strong, straight nose. He was beautiful.

And he had silver eyes.

Not blue-gray, not gray. Silver. I stared in shock at them, and then he was gone, back out the door even as Mrs. Jones said, "Hold on one second and I'll get your schedule from your file so you'll be ready to start your classes."

"Well," she said, when she returned and saw he'd left, "I guess he'll be back in a second. I'll call your grandmother in the meantime. Holler if he does come back in, all right?"

I nodded, but he didn't come back. I would have thought I dreamed him, except Mrs. Jones left his schedule on the counter and I got up to look at it, curious even though I had no reason to be.

He was new, and his name was Ben Dusic. He lived out near where I did.

Where I had.

He'd lived in a place called Little Falls before, a place I'd never heard of, but now he lived with Louis Dusic, who was listed as his great-uncle.

Mrs. Jones said, "Avery, I thought I told you to have a seat." Frowning, she picked up Ben's schedule before I could read more. "He didn't come back?"

"No," I said, and remembered Dad saying something about Louis, our nearest neighbor, having someone—family—moving in. He and Mom and me were supposed to go out and say hello soon. Mom was going to make banana bread.

I had said I wasn't going. I had no interest in meeting any relative of Louis's. He was as old as Renee and always acted as if he wanted to be anywhere but talking to you.

"Sit down and wait for your grandma," Mrs. Jones said again, and I did.

Ben didn't come back. I wondered what he'd heard about my parents. I figured it was everything, and wondered if he wished he lived somewhere else now.

Renee came in after a little while and waved at Mrs. Jones, who said, "Any news?"

Renee shook her head and looked at me. "Ready to go?"

I nodded. I got up, I walked outside, and I got in the car.

"That bad?" Renee said as we pulled away from the school.

"I was supposed to draw apples," I said, and Renee nodded like she knew what I meant. It made me think of Dad, of how you could say anything to him and he would do the same thing. He was always willing to wait until you could find the words for what you wanted to say.

I looked at her for a moment.

"Why are you so angry at him?" I finally said.

"He could have done anything after college," she said slowly. "But he didn't. He came back here. I hated that."

"You're here."

"Yes," she said. "I'm still here."

The sorrow in her voice was as real as the anger I'd heard at the funeral, and I looked out the window. I could see the road that led into the forest, that led to *our* house, to me and Mom and Dad. To before.

We didn't turn down it.

three

That night, I dreamed my parents and I were having dinner. Mom had made chicken potpie, the crust curling over the edge of the bowls she'd baked it in, and Dad picked all the carrots out of his and grinned at her when she said, "Well, I like them," and ate them off his plate, her hand bumping his arm.

"Ugh," I said, embarrassed by their easy affection but also sort of proud of it too. My parents loved each other in a way I never saw shared by any other parents.

"I made chocolate pie," Mom said, and I got up and took it out of the fridge. There was a crack down the center and I showed it to Mom.

"It happens," she said. "Pies are tricky things."

"Like life," Dad said.

Mom smiled in agreement and said, "Avery, will you get a knife to cut it? You can have the first piece."

I went over to the wooden block where all the knives rested, their handles sticking out, and then everything went dark.

"Dad, the power's gone out *again*," I said, and bent down to get a flashlight. The power was always going out, and we were forever at the mercy of the one line that ran into the forest to be turned back on when it went down.

I couldn't find a flashlight. Not one, when I knew we had at least three. I couldn't even find the cabinet under the sink. My hand cut through air and I reached for the counter to steady myself.

My hand slid through air again, through nothing.

"Mom?" I said, and then, "Dad?" but they didn't reply.

They didn't reply, and I couldn't see anything. I couldn't even hear them, and then I—

I wasn't in the kitchen anymore.

I was outside. I could see the shapes of the trees and I could hear them too, rustling together like a whisper. They were there, all around me. I could even smell them, their rich pine and dirt scent, sharp and bracing.

Why was I outside? How had that happened? When? Why?

I turned to go back to the house, but it wasn't there. Nothing was there.

Nothing but darkness.

"Dad! Mom!" I said, but it didn't come out as a cry. It

came out as a whisper, and I couldn't make my voice louder, I couldn't make it heard.

And then I felt something slide across my feet.

I tried to move away, but then realized I was near the house. I knew the trees that were close by it; I recognized the little bumps that made up the rise and subtle fall of the forest I walked through every single day.

I could even see my shadow again, lit by the house, and now there was something sticky on my hand.

I looked and saw a smear of chocolate on one of my fingers. I hoped Mom wasn't mad at me for tasting the pie before I cut it and wanted to go back inside to see her and Dad.

I *had* to.

I started to move, but the tree I was near held me, its branches catching me, and something was soaking through my sneakers, strangely warm against my feet.

I looked down, and saw I was standing in a river of red.

It was deep, dark brown red, blood red, and it was running fast and hard and covered my shoes, rising up over my ankles.

I knew what was happening then. I knew I had to find my parents and I tried to turn, tried to look for them, but it was dark again, so dark, and I couldn't see a thing.

I screamed for them again but nothing came out, like the darkness had taken me away; like I was outside, but not in the outside where they were, not like I was

anywhere they were, and I felt rough wood, tree bark, under my cheek, and I was lying down somehow.

I was shivering and the red was everywhere now, all over me, and I was going to see, I was going to see—

Silver, gleaming cold and precise. Silver, moving and slicing down, down, down.

I woke up screaming.

"We—we were eating dinner," I told Renee when she came running in to me, turning on a light and chasing away the dark. "I went to get a knife for the pie and then I wasn't . . . I was outside and Mom and Dad weren't there. They weren't with me, and then there was blood and—"

"Avery," Renee said. "Avery, Avery." She grabbed my hands in hers, squeezed hard.

I stopped talking and waited for her to tell me she'd call Ron, that she knew he needed to hear this, but she kept holding my hands tight, her eyes huge and sad as she looked at me.

"I remembered something," I said, my voice rising a little. "We were having pie—no, we were going to have it, and I went to get a knife and then I wasn't inside anymore, and they—"

"Avery," Renee said again, and stood up, keeping her grip on my hands. I rose up too, my whole body shaking from what I'd seen—what I'd remembered—and then I saw myself in the dresser mirror.

Something had happened to my hair.

It was the same length it always was, a little below my shoulders, and was still the same reddish brown that my mother's hair had been except for one piece.

There was a section of hair right by my face, sliding across my cheek, curling near my mouth, that was pure red. Not a happy red, the cheery color of holidays. Not pretty red, like the glow of a sunrise or sunset.

It was dark red. Brown red. Blood red.

"I—" I said, and stared at myself in the mirror. Saw Renee was staring at me too.

"You had a nightmare," she said, "a bad dream, that's all," but her voice was shaking and we both knew I hadn't had a dream at all.

We both knew something had happened.

But what was it?

I'd remembered eating dinner with my parents. I could still smell the chicken potpie. Still see Dad and Mom smiling at each other. I could still see the crack in the chocolate pie.

But what happened after that? Why did I end up outside? Why—?

I remembered the silver again, that graceful, sudden, and swift arc, that noiseless, brutal blur, and knew it was what had taken my parents away.

I knew it was death.

"I remembered seeing something silver, something very strange, and I think that's what killed Mom and Dad.

I don't know why it came, I don't know why it wanted to hurt them, I just . . . why did it come? Why?"

I was shaking so hard I could hardly stand and Renee held me up, turned me away from the mirror.

"Okay, shhhh, shhhh," she said. She led me downstairs and made me drink a glass of milk thick with strawberry syrup, something she used to make when I was little, back before I stopped seeing her. It didn't taste good—it tasted fake, not like real strawberries at all—but I was thirsty and the more I drank, the better I felt.

"We should call Ron," I said when I was done.

"No."

"No?"

"No," Renee said again. "You had a dream. That's not—it's not real."

"I *remembered* something," I said. "We were having dinner and then I—I saw silver, I saw blood. And I know that's when they died."

"The police . . . honey, they already know that you and your parents were eating dinner," she said, looking at the kitchen table. "If you remember more, we'll call Ron right away, I promise."

"You think the silver and everything I've said was a dream? You think I—?" I paused, remembered the red warmth in my shoes, how it rose.

What it was.

I knew what was real even if no one else did, and now

I had to know what—and it was a *what*—had killed my parents. I had to be sure before I said anything else. As soon as I remembered everything, things would—

Things would still never be the same again.

I didn't go back to sleep that night.

Renee didn't either. We sat in the kitchen together, silent, and watched the sun rise through the sliding glass door that looked out into the woods.

"My hair," I said when it was light out, when I could see that what I'd glimpsed in the mirror before was real. "Why did it change color like this? What's happening to me?"

I waited for Renee to say something, but she didn't, not for a long time, and when she finally did speak, all she said was, "I don't know."

She sounded nervous, and I watched her look into the forest. I saw her eyes close in something that looked like memory. Like regret.

I shuddered, my teeth clacking together, and she got up and came over to me.

"You will be safe, I swear," she said. It sounded like a plea.

It sounded like she was as scared as I was.

four

I could have stayed home that day, and maybe I should have. But after that dream—after those memories—and the worry in Renee's voice, I needed to get away. And since I couldn't run from myself, I could at least get away from her house. As for what I knew, and how I knew it—well, that didn't solve anything at all.

I walked by Kirsta on my way to first period. She saw my hair and stopped, stared at me. She knew I'd never dye my hair. She knew I'd have no idea how to do it. But I didn't expect her to say what she did.

"You're cursed," she said, and then said it again, louder, as people looked at her and then me. I could see fear in everyone's eyes, saw them look at her and watch her mouth move. I saw them think about what had happened to me and believe her. I watched her face light up as people turned to her, as they listened to her.

The worst part was, I didn't think she was wrong. I felt cursed.

I knew something was wrong with me. Whatever I'd seen, it had somehow done this to me. It had taken my parents and now—the blood red strand of hair had fallen across my face. I pushed it back behind my ear and thought of that gleaming, brutal silver.

I had to find out what had killed my parents and left me here, strange and lost and broken.

And now I was marked too.

I went into the bathroom and stood by the sinks, looking at my hair. Some girls came in and I watched them look at me and then turn away.

Cursed.

I got through the day somehow, and then, in Art, I saw the guy from yesterday. Ben.

He was standing at the easel next to mine when I walked in. I hadn't heard any talk about him during the day because I hadn't been part of any conversations, but I could see how all the girls were looking at him.

He was still wearing moccasins, something else no other guy would, but they looked right on him, the ties that wrapped around his legs looking natural when they would have looked stupid and fake on anyone else.

He had been staring at the piece of blank paper on his easel, but he turned when I walked toward him, and his hands clenched into fists by his sides.

So he'd heard about me, then.

He stiffened as I walked past him and I knew he'd heard everything, that he thought what everyone else did, that I was the girl whose parents had been murdered, that I was the girl who remembered nothing even though she was found with the bodies.

I was the girl who had hair like blood.

He started to move away, heading for the other side of the room, for an easel far away from mine, but our teacher said, "All right, get started," and he stopped as everyone around us started to draw.

And then he looked at me.

He looked at me, and for a moment it was like he *had* to look at me. Like he *wanted* to look at me.

But then he looked away, his mouth set in a thin line.

"You loved them," he said, and his voice was low and soft. Sad. But it was beautiful too, as beautiful as he was.

"Yes," I said, somehow knowing he meant my parents and surprised he'd spoken to me at all. Surprised by how sad he sounded.

"Your hair—when my parents died, my great-uncle's co—his hair turned white overnight from grief. And I . . . I know what it's like to lose everything you had, to lose your whole life."

I didn't want to touch my hair then, didn't want to call attention to the strand, but of course it fell free, swung blood red across my face and snared on my mouth.

I pulled it back, shoved it behind my ear, but Ben stared at it and then he stared at me. His mouth parted as he did, his eyes widening slightly.

He stared at me, and he was so close I could see that his eyes were truly silver, no blue or green or gray anywhere in them, only small flecks of gold that somehow blended in and made his eyes gleam.

Silver.

"Your eyes," I whispered, and he stiffened, then looked away, turning so all I could see was his back. I heard someone giggle and then someone else said, "Ben, do you want to come over here?" I had to get out of there.

I had to—

He had silver eyes.

I grabbed my things, fumbling with them, and he looked at me again as I left. His eyes locked with mine, staring, and I realized they weren't silver at all. They were brown, ordinary brown.

I fled anyway, heading for the office and Mrs. Jones. For Renee, who came and got me again. As I waited for her, I wondered if I was going crazy. I wondered why Ben had spoken to me.

I wondered why I'd seen his eyes so wrong.

five

I'm thinking of building a porch," Renee said as we drove back to her house. We were taking the long way, driving through town, Woodlake's postcard-perfect main street gleaming with the police station sitting just off to the side of the one tree left from where the first people to settle in Woodlake had built their homes. My father wrote about that tree every year on Woodlake's "anniversary" day, when all the town businesses had sales and the town council had a picnic that everyone went to.

I remembered last year's picnic; how my father had stiffened when he saw Renee and then relaxed when she turned back to the conversation she'd been having and said, "No, I don't know if we'll see the Thantos family this year. They don't usually come. Louis? No, I don't think he comes to these things either."

"You could say hello," Mom had whispered to Dad.

"She's not going to live forever, John, and I know you love her."

"I'm tired of not being what she wants me to be," Dad said, and then went off to talk to some little kids who were poking the memorial tree. I watched him shape his hands in his air, explaining how much time it took for the tree to grow that big, how once where we stood was nothing but trees. How we needed to respect all they did for us, how we needed to see their beauty.

"Hello there, strangers," Renee said, and I watched Mom plaster a smile on her face.

"Hello, Renee," she said. "What did you bring to the picnic?"

"Apple pie," Renee said, and looked at me. "Hello, Avery."

"Hi, Renee," I said. "I gotta go put this potato salad down."

I knew Mom wouldn't be happy about having to talk to Renee by herself, but she could handle it. I never knew what to do around Renee.

When I was little, I'd loved her so much. I loved her house, which looked like a real house, with an upstairs and a downstairs, and not like the weird thing my dad had built, a series of rooms that he'd added on one at a time as we needed more space.

Renee had walls that all looked the same, that were all painted white. None of our walls matched. Even in my bedroom I had one wall made of wood that someone had

tossed at a construction site because of a crack, one made of part of a trailer my father had bought at an auction, and a third made out of glass, a huge window that looked out into the woods and that always woke me up in the morning because the sun rose right through it. There was no fourth wall, just the doorway to the next room, which was a pantry Dad built for Mom right after I'd turned two, and so I slept next to jars of Mom's canned tomatoes and peas and wild berry jam—the jars for us separated from the jars she'd made to sell.

Renee's house was nothing like that, and when I went to see her she'd give me pizza from the only restaurant in town, Bessie's, and the one time Mom and Dad let me spend the night, I'd taken a shower and thought it was like what being in the ocean must be like, a strong spray of water washing over me.

"I love your shower, Grandma," I'd told her as she made pancakes the next morning. "It's like the sea."

"The sea?" she'd said, and I told her how it felt so different from our shower at home, which ran off solar panels and where the water came out slowly, like a stream.

"A stream shower?" she said. "That sounds like your father. Oh, honey, you eat up, all right?"

Dad and her had a huge fight about it when he came to get me, Dad saying, "I'm not depriving Avery, Mother. We have a bathroom, we have a shower. We just don't waste water like you do."

"I didn't say you were depriving her, I said it might be nice to think about giving her a little normalcy, John. Not everyone is cut out for a life in the woods, for a life that's so . . ."

"So what, Mother?"

"Isolated," Grandma finally said. "I see how beautiful the woods are, and I understand the appeal, but—"

"No, you don't," Dad said, and Grandma bit her lip like she might cry, then saw me and said, "Look at you. What big eyes you have, Avery! Come on in here and give me a kiss good-bye."

I did, and we kept going to her house, but it got so every time we went over there, my father and grandmother fought, and I started to hate hearing, "It's time to go to Grandma's house." I started to hate how upset my father got when her house came into view, how my mother would sit looking nervous and trapped during meals we shared, and how Grandma would always ask me if I was having fun, as if listening to people yell while I ate could ever be fun.

And then, when I was ten, my father stopped talking to Renee at all.

Ron Jericho, who was the sheriff even then, came out to our house one night and spent a long time talking to Dad, the two of them walking around outside. I could see them out my window while I worked on the fractions Mom had asked me to do.

As Ron talked, my father nodded like he agreed, but his whole body grew stiffer and stiffer.

Finally he said something, and Ron shook his head, smiling. His smile faded at my father's reply, but he held out his hand for my father to shake.

Dad didn't take it. He just turned around and came back to the house.

"My mother called Ron," I heard him say later that night, after I was supposed to be in bed. "She called Ron and told him I should be living in town. So he came out here and said he'd talk to his friend, Steve, and see if he was interested in buying the house and our land. I can't believe she did this!"

"John," Mom said, "she might have said something to Ron, but you don't know what it was, and Steve is awfully pushy."

"This isn't Ron. I know it. It isn't even Steve Browning, as horrible as he is. It's her. She never ... she didn't even love my father," Dad said. "She had to marry him because of me, and they came back here and they were—" He broke off.

"They were never happy. Never. It was like part of her was just gone," he said after a moment. "And she won't see me for who I am. No matter what I do, it's all about what she wants me to be."

"John," my mother said again, her voice softer, and I crept back to my room.

I only saw my grandmother in town after that, and I didn't call her Grandma anymore. The icy silence that was around whenever she and Dad saw each other made the word too weird to say. So I called her Renee like my mother did, like she was any other adult I knew.

"You—I'm Grandma," she said the first time I ran into her in town and called her by her name, but I'd shaken my head, angry and scared. She said, "Well, then, all right," and never said another word about it.

I'd stopped thinking about her so much over the years, although I sometimes wondered how she was. It got easy to never say more than hello to her, to never do more than look at her house if we happened to drive by it.

And then my parents—then that night happened—and now I was living with Renee.

My grandmother, and a total stranger.

"So, what do you think?" Renee said now. "How does a porch sound? I'm going to put it off the kitchen, so you can open the sliding glass door and walk right out onto it. I've drawn plans and ordered the wood."

"Who's building it?"

"I am."

"You?"

"Yes," she said, and her voice was sad. "I can build things, Avery."

We passed by the road that led into the forest. The road that I knew well. The road that led home.

It was empty, like usual—the only cars I ever saw on it were Mom's or Dad's or sometimes, very rarely, Louis's—and now the sunlight glinted off it, showed—

Showed someone walking along it.

Showed someone looking at our car.

It was Ben.

I almost raised a hand, like I was going to wave or something, but managed to stop myself just in time.

I still stared, though. At least we were far enough away that he wouldn't know it was me.

He was still looking at the car though, and somehow it seemed like he did know who was in it.

Like somehow he saw me.

"What are you looking at?" Renee said. I shook my head.

"As soon as Ron says I can, I'll take you out to the house," she told me, and I wondered why she'd never been there. She'd never come out into the woods, not even before she and Dad had stopped talking.

Why?

I started to ask her, but then caught a glimpse of my hair in the mirror. I stared at that blood red strand, and realized that now it . . .

Now it shone.

It shone deep, blood red.

I swallowed and tucked it behind one ear, but when I was back at Renee's, when I was up in the guest room

that was now my room, I went and got a pair of scissors and cut it away.

I didn't look at it once. I just cut and pretended it had never been there at all.

six

Renee must have noticed my hair at dinner that night, but she didn't say anything about it. She just showed me the drawings she'd done for the porch.

"I didn't know you liked the forest so much," I said. The porch would look right into the trees, right into the woods.

She smiled at me sadly.

"How could you?" she said, and I thought of all those years we'd never spoken, all those years I'd seen her and been careful to treat her like she was no one special to me.

I'd hurt her, I realized, and I think I'd always known that. But it was easy not to see it when I'd had Mom and Dad. When I knew my world and understood it.

I didn't understand anything now.

"I'll help you with it, if you want," I said, and Renee smiled at me, a real smile, one that reminded me of Dad's, that made my eyes sting. I blinked hard and looked down at her drawings.

I tried to picture myself on the porch because I lived here now.

This—now—was my life.

I missed my parents so much then. It wasn't an ache. It wasn't something that simple. It wasn't even a longing, a wishing. It was *me*, it was all I was, and I said I was tired and went to bed, lay in the guest room, wide awake and lonely.

"Avery, go outside now," I heard Mom whisper, and sat up, dazed. I'd been in the place where I was almost—but not quite—asleep, and had I heard her? Was I remembering something else?

I closed my eyes and thought of her. Of Mom. Of that night, and the darkness that was my memory.

I didn't hear anything else. I didn't remember anything else.

I rolled onto my side, frustrated, and then got up and opened the window. I listened to the sounds of the night, relaxed into their familiar hold. There was even the faint, low howl of a wolf in the distance, a cry I'd heard so often at home, sometimes so loud it would wake me in the middle of the night, the full moon shining in through my curtains and the skin on my arms prickling at the way the wolves' song seemed to make the moon pulse and glow bright like the sun.

The wolf—and it was one wolf, one lone, soft, crooning cry—howled again. I looked at the moon and tried again to go back to that night. To that black hole in my mind.

I thought of the forest instead. Our forest, but I couldn't even go there. I wasn't even allowed to go home again.

The wolf's cry came once more, longer this time, sadder.

I got up. I pulled on some clothes, and then went downstairs, outside. I went out into the night, the grass wet and cold even through my sneakers. The stars, once I moved away from Renee's yard lights, shone bright, almost like at home.

I looked at the forest, at the dark trees, and I didn't hesitate at all. I walked straight to them.

I walked to where I wanted to be.

seven

The forest was cooler than Renee's backyard, the trees creating a canopy that held the dark tight, but I didn't mind. I knew this. I knew the forest.

I sat down by a tree and looked up at the sky. There were the stars, shining bright, the Milky Way a shimmering cluster all around them.

When I was little, I was scared of only one thing. I was scared I would be taken into the sky, that somehow I'd be pulled up there, that all the bright stars Dad and Mom showed me would want to take me away from home and the woods that held me tight.

Now I wished the stars *would* take me away. I wanted to be absorbed by them. To be pulled away by them, to see—

To see Mom and Dad again.

I looked away from the stars then and into the woods,

mapped the way home in my mind. I could make the walk easily from here. I could be home soon.

I could be in my house, in my room.

But no one would be there, and I—

I closed my eyes because I smelled blood and saw silver, so bright, so strange, and—

The wolf howled yet again, closer now, and I opened my eyes, shuddering.

There were stories about Woodlake's wolves, of course. There were stories about everything in Woodlake. The most famous one about the wolves said the whole town was built because a deal was made between the first settlers and the wolves, a deal that gave the wolves brides, only—naturally the wolves in the story weren't normal wolves. They were different. They could look human. Were part human.

Crimes had even been blamed on them back when the town was first built, back when Ron's great-great-grandfather was sheriff—Woodlake never messed with a good thing—but, as Dad would say, the truth was always less interesting.

I heard rustling then, the sound of someone moving through the forest.

I should have gotten up, but I was so surprised to hear the sounds of someone else that I didn't. No one was ever in this part of the forest at night except for my parents and me. In all the years we'd gone out at night,

we'd never seen another person, not even the Thantos family, and so I stayed right where I was, figuring I'd see a rabbit or maybe a deer.

And then I saw Ben Dusic thread his way between two trees, his skin pale in the moonlight.

He was even more beautiful in the moonlight than he was at school. I hadn't thought that was possible.

And there I was, in a T-shirt and old sweatpants and my ratty sneakers, sitting hunched against a tree in the middle of the night. I so didn't want him to see me, especially not like this. I just wanted to be alone.

I couldn't help but look at him, though. Not because of how he looked, but because he was someone who clearly knew the woods too.

He moved effortlessly, gently pushing away branches that would have caught me, and then he stilled. His head turned in my direction.

It was dark. The moon wasn't full and my hair was dark and I was leaning against a tree, its branches hiding me. He wouldn't notice me. He couldn't.

"Avery?" he said, and somehow, someway, he'd seen me.

eight

"Avery," he said again, not a question this time, and then he was there, right in front of me, kneeling down near where I was sitting.

"What are you doing out here?" He sounded almost scared.

"I live near here," I said. After all, it was true. Now. But it hurt to say, and my eyes stung.

"You're upset," Ben said. "What's wrong?"

He was being nice, but it was like the words were torn from him, like he had to say them and didn't want to, and his face—his face was so beautiful but so—he wore a strange mixture of concern, anger, and fear.

"I'm fine," I said, not because I'd had plenty of pity—although I had—but because I could practically feel him vibrating with some strange tension and it was clear I wasn't who he wanted—or expected—to see right now.

"You're upset," he said again. His voice got softer, less angry and more concerned. "Did something happen to you?"

"Other than my parents being murdered?"

He rocked back on his heels like I'd hit him, and then shook his head, his dark hair gleaming in the moonlight.

"Louis told me about them," he said after a moment. "He said they were nice. That they loved the woods like few people do. He was sad when he heard the news." He paused. "He's still very sad. And I—I'm sorry too."

"So you really do live with Louis?" I said, thinking of the quiet old man who'd lived down the road from us, a man I didn't ever even remember once speaking to for more than a few moments. I didn't think he'd even ever met the Thantos family, who were the only other people living as far out in the woods as we did.

Dad thought Louis was someone who had lost everything he loved and had moved into the woods to escape that loss. Mom thought the same, and the few times we saw him she'd always invite him to come and have dinner with us.

He never came, but I remembered him, not because of how he looked, which was average, old and sad-eyed, but because of how quiet he was. He had this way of taking conversations—even with Dad, who could always get anyone to talk—and ending them with a word or two. Politely, but still, it was clear that he was done talking.

"Yes," Ben said. "I—we're still getting to know each other."

"It's hard with family that you don't know like maybe you should."

Ben nodded, and it was like . . . he was looking at me like he saw something in me. Saw something . . . I don't know. Something he had to see, that he couldn't turn away from.

No one had ever looked at me like that.

"You know the woods," I said, because I couldn't ask about how he was looking at me even though part of me longed to.

Ben blinked and looked away from me, his fists clenching and unclenching by his sides.

"Yes," he said again, and stood up, backed away. "This forest is amazing. And you—you changed your hair."

"How did you know that?" I said. "It's so dark I wouldn't think you could see it."

"I see it," he said softly. "I see you. But why are you out here now?"

"I heard a wolf, and I—"

"You heard a wolf? How could you hear that? You live in town."

"I'm used to hearing them, so I guess I know what to listen for," I said. "I live—lived—near your great-uncle, remember? The woods are deeper there, without so much—" I gestured toward town, toward Renee's house off in the distance.

"Right," Ben said, standing up. "I need to go."

"Oh, okay," I said, and sank back against the tree, ready to watch him go.

But he didn't leave. He just stood there.

"Are you all right?" I said after a moment.

He looked at me again, a hot, glazed look in his eyes, and said, "No."

"Do you want me to—? I could go get Renee, and she could drive you home." As soon as I said it I knew he would refuse.

And he did, he acted like I hadn't spoken at all and said, "You can't remember what happened to your parents, but you want to. You need to."

I didn't know how he knew that, but he did know it. He sounded so sure I felt my eyes burn again, wrapped my hands tight around my knees.

"Yes," I whispered, and he came close again, sank down beside me. He smelled like the forest, like night, rich earth, and darkness. My skin prickled.

"I've lost people I loved too, and I think you always carry it with you. I'm sorry for that, and for what you don't know. I can feel how much you want to."

"Feel it?" I said, and he shifted, said, "Heard about it. I heard about everything that happened."

That made sense but I . . .

For some reason, I didn't believe him. I don't know why, but I knew he had felt my sadness out here in the woods and had come over. Come to see me.

"I don't mean to bother you," I whispered, and he looked at me. I looked at his feet. He was wearing his moccasins, the edges dark with soil.

"You aren't," he said. "I wish . . . I have to go now. You'll go back to your grandmother's house, right?"

It sounded, weirdly, like an order, not a question, and for a second, just a second, I wanted to say *yes* and go, walk back to Renee's house.

And then I remembered that it wasn't the Dark Ages and I could do what I wanted. That all I had left was myself and Renee, and I had left her house because I felt so alone. Because I wanted to be here in the forest.

"I will when I'm ready to go," I said, and he blinked at me. I watched the sweep of his lashes, dark like his hair, and his eyes—they looked silver again for a moment—gleamed in the moonlight.

"You don't want to go?"

"Not yet."

"Then I'll wait with you." The words sounded so formal. Forced.

"No, thank you," I said, just as polite, but he sat down and didn't move, sat right by me and looked out into the forest, the dark, with me.

"I'm not making you stay, you know," I said after a moment, confused, and he looked at me again.

"No," he said. "I want to stay." It sounded torn from him.

It sounded scared, and I had been going to school

long enough to understand how guys looked at girls, how they spoke to them when they wanted them, and he wasn't talking like that, but his voice was—

His voice was full of feeling, and he was still looking at me.

"Why?" I said, my voice cracking. No one other than Renee wanted to be anywhere near me.

"Avery," he said, moving toward me, and he was so close now, he was right next to me, his breath fanning across my mouth, and his own was tight, a muscle in his jaw jumping, and I—

What was going on inside me, in my heart, scared me.

"I'm going home now," I said and got up. Boys like Ben didn't want to kiss me. I was dreaming, I was sure of it, and I'd wake up and find myself in bed in Renee's guest room, the whole thing a sad, strange dream.

"Avery," Ben said, and it wasn't a dream. He was here. He was real. This was happening. I turned back toward him.

"You need to be careful in the forest," he said, and he was still close, so close.

And then he was gone. Just like that, he disappeared into the forest and I was standing there, not in a dream but wishing I was in one. In a dream I wouldn't feel so strange.

In a dream, he'd kiss me.

nine

The next day, I didn't have to worry about seeing Ben. School was closed because of a teachers' workday, and I was glad. I kept thinking I couldn't have seen Ben last night, that I must have dreamed it all.

But then I woke up and saw my sweatpants stained with dirt, and knew it wasn't a dream. It had all happened.

Ben had talked to me. He had looked at me like he—

He had looked at me like he wanted me, even though he'd seemed to want to get away from me before.

He'd also told me to be careful in the forest.

Why? He was new, he didn't know the forest like I did. He couldn't. But then why had he sounded so sure?

It was a relief to eat breakfast with Renee, to drive out of town to the nearest big hardware store and pick up things she needed to build the porch, to come back and eat lunch and see a pile of wood delivered, watch the men who unloaded it glance at us, an old woman and a girl, and clearly wonder what we were doing.

"Did you sleep all right last night?" Renee said as they were leaving.

"I . . . sure," I said.

Renee looked at me. "I heard you get up. If you ever want to talk, we can. I know it's been years, but I—" She broke off as a car pulled into the driveway, a bright red sports car.

"Hello, Steve," she said, and Steve got out of the car and said, "Hear you're building something."

"Did you now?" Renee said, making Steve smile. The sun gleamed off the tag on his chest, the one that said STEVE BROWNING, REAL ESTATE AGENT.

"Avery," he said, glancing at me. "How are you?"

I shrugged.

He sighed, and then looked at Renee. "Can we talk?"

"Sure," Renee said. "I'm building a porch though, not thinking about moving, all right?"

He laughed and said, "I think the porch will look real nice, but I actually came out here for another reason. Can we talk in private?"

"All right," Renee said. "Avery, you want to go on inside and get Steve a glass of water?"

As if I was a little kid and not seventeen. As if I didn't

have a right to know what they were talking about. As if I didn't know Steve was there because of my parents' land. Steve sold houses, but he was also a developer. He'd planned all the new subdivisions that had slowly started to pop up around town.

"I'd like to stay if you're going to talk about my parents or their land," I said.

"I actually came because I ran into Ron in town," he said. "I wanted to say I was sorry there wasn't any news about what happened." He stuck his hands in his pockets and looked at me. "Avery," he continued, his voice kind, "I'll be honest with you. Ron says you're the best hope they've got, and he said if you can remember anything about that night, anything at all—"

Silver, gleaming . . .

Ben's eyes were silver.

I felt a shudder crawl up my spine.

Ben had been in the woods last night. Told me I should be careful in them.

But Ben didn't even know my parents. He'd only known who I was because people at school told him.

And the silver I'd seen the night my parents died was . . .

It wasn't human. It had been too strange. Too fast-moving. Too brutal.

Too evil.

"Avery," Steve said again, and he and Renee were standing right next to me, both of them looking at me with concern.

"Are you all right?" Renee said, putting one arm around me.

The last person who'd held me was my mother. It was right before dinner and she'd pulled me close, said, "You're still on table-setting duty, so get to it," and then kissed the side of my head.

I'd groaned and pulled away. I hadn't wanted to set the table. I hadn't been that interested in a hug. I could get them anytime.

Or at least, that's what I'd thought.

"I miss them," I said. "I miss them and I want to know why someone would kill them. I want to know but I can't—" My voice cracked, and Renee pulled me closer against her.

"I'm really sorry I'm not out here with better news," Steve said. "I know Ron feels the same way, and he told me that anything you saw, no matter how small, could help find who did this."

Avery, go outside. Go out to that patch of mushrooms we found yesterday and pick some, all right? I'll make omelets in the morning.

Now? Mom, it's dark out and we haven't even had pie, so—

You've been sneaking pie already, sweetheart. You've got

*some on your hand. We'll have more, but now—Avery, take
your bag and go. Please?*

Is everything all right?

Avery, please go.

All right, fine, I'm going. I was just asking.

"She sent me out to get mushrooms," I whispered, and
Renee stiffened. Just slightly, but I felt it.

And Steve . . . Steve took a step back, his eyes wide.

"Mushrooms?" he said.

"For omelets," I said. "It was just after dinner, right
when it was starting to get dark, but I wouldn't have
taken a flashlight. I knew the way."

"And then what?"

"Steve," Renee said, but he turned away from her and
looked at me.

"Avery, then what?"

I tried to picture myself going outside. Leaving Mom
and Dad behind in the house. But I couldn't see it. I
couldn't see anything. I just remembered Mom telling me
to go and get mushrooms.

And I remembered the blood. The flash of silver. Opening my eyes and not knowing where I was, seeing Renee
looking at me and hearing her say, "Avery, oh, Avery," so
sadly that I knew there was a horrible reason why I was
wherever I was.

Why when I said, "Where are Mom and Dad?" her face
crumpled.

Why when I looked down at my hands I remembered the red, rust-colored flecks dug deep into the cuticles on my fingers, dug deep under the beds of my fingernails.

"Blood," I whispered now. I remember seeing blood on me and knowing—*knowing*—

"All right, Avery, all right," Renee said, trying to pull me closer, but it was awkward—a one-arm embrace, clumsy and disjointed.

And it was all I had. I breathed in deep, wishing for the fruit-scented smell of my mother, or the deep-woods scent of my father, but Renee didn't smell like that at all. She didn't smell like either of them. She smelled like coffee and shampoo and a little like the wood we'd been looking at all morning.

It wasn't enough, I wasn't enough, I couldn't *remember*, not even when I tried thinking about different things; of places, of smells, of anything.

I squeezed my eyes shut, trying not to cry. A few tears leaked out anyway.

"You're sure that's all you remember?" Steve said, and Renee said, "Steve, since when did you join the police force?" her voice crisp.

Steve cleared his throat and said, "I got carried away there, Renee. I'm sorry. Everyone in town is upset over this. And it sounded like Avery might have remembered something, given us all a reason to hope that this can be solved and put to rest."

I pulled away and shook my head.

"It's all darkness," I said to Steve. "I don't remember who found me, or even Ron coming at first. I know he did because Renee told me, but I can't see it. I just remember him taking me away. Seeing..." I broke off.

Some hope I was. Someone had killed my parents, torn them apart while I was off getting mushrooms and I—

I froze.

The mushrooms. I hadn't thought about them before.

"Did the police find them?" I said, and Steve blinked at me.

"Your parents? Avery, you know they did. You were at the funeral, and—"

"No," I said, shaking my head. "Mushrooms. Did Ron say anything to you about finding anything around my parents when you saw him? Did he say anything about finding something around me?"

"Oh. No, nothing like that," Steve said. His voice was very kind.

"But I..." I trailed off. I didn't remember actually getting mushrooms, just Mom telling me to go get them. I didn't even remember leaving the house. But I would have left to get the mushrooms.

What had happened to the mushrooms? Had I never gotten them?

What if I had?

What had happened to me?

"I really could use a glass of water, Avery," Steve said, his voice still so kind, but I knew he hadn't believed anything I said. He thought my mind was still a blank.

But I'd seen more.

Silver, moving with inhuman grace.

Silver, and blood flowing everywhere.

I opened my mouth, then closed it, and headed to the house to get Steve some water because I already knew what he'd think if I told him about the silver. I'd seen his face when I told him about the mushrooms, and he hadn't believed me at all.

Besides, Steve wasn't someone my parents would have wanted me talking to. Ron and Dad had been friends since they were little, and although they didn't agree about a lot of things, one thing they had agreed on was that whispers about the forest were nothing but gossip, while Steve was always quick to say things like, "Well, you never know with those unchecked woods. Development is key to Woodlake's future." I knew Dad only ever tolerated being around him at all because of Ron.

"Wolves are wolves," my father had said last year when I'd asked him about a story I'd heard at school. Kirsta had told me that the first settlers in Woodlake survived only because they agreed to send two girls out into the woods on their own. That there were men living

out there who were part wolf and that they wanted brides.

"Someone can't be part human any more than I can be part hamster," Dad had told me. "It's just a story that someone came up with back when the wolf population swelled for a few years, and people got scared because they'd sometimes come into town. There's a picture of one wolf on Main Street in the newspaper's archives. I'll bring it home for you to see."

Now, in Renee's kitchen, I turned on the faucet and filled a glass.

It was clear and matched all the others Renee had. Her glasses weren't like ours, a mix of colors and styles my parents had picked up from yard sales or even found tossed into the woods.

Dad had hated people dumping stuff in the woods even more than he'd hated what he'd called "that old wolf story." He had brought the photo home for me to see like he'd said he would. It was very old, yellowing and crumbling at the edges, and it was of one wolf walking down Main Street, not frightening at all.

"Most likely got turned around and ended up in town. Scared people silly, though, and that's how the story about the wolves got started."

"The wolf looks scared," I said. "Lonely."

"Wolves aren't people, Avery," he said. "You know that. It was probably confused, though."

I looked at the photo again and thought that wolf looked something much worse than confused. It really did look scared. Terrified, even. But I didn't tell Dad that.

And I wouldn't tell Steve about what I'd seen because he wouldn't believe me. I needed to remember everything and so I stood there in the kitchen, glass in hand, and tried. Not like before, not by trying to push myself back into that night, but by simply thinking about them. About me and Mom and Dad and how we were.

I remembered a million moments, a million things I'd taken for granted, and it made me feel loved, safe.

And then I remembered Mom's voice telling me to go out to get mushrooms again, and really focused on that moment, that memory. I imagined myself in the house and when she told me to go, I would have—I would have—

Nothing.

No, I had to keep going. What would have happened next?

I probably would have put on my shoes and gone out. And I did have my sneakers on when the police found me.

But I didn't remember putting them on at all.

I sighed, angry and frustrated with how my own mind seemed to be working against me, and went back outside.

I'd been inside for longer than I supposed because Renee and Steve were standing by his car now, Steve

leaning against it. Neither of them looked very happy, and as I got closer I heard Steve say, "Renee, I know you hated John living out there and with what happened, the memories—well, they can't be pleasant. So why not let me take it all off your hands and—" He broke off and smiled at me as I gave him the glass of water.

"You're serious?" Renee said, her voice thick with emotion. "I can't believe you came out here to ask me this, Steve. John loved that place."

"But you didn't, and after what happened—"

"That place?" I said, cutting him off. "You mean our house?"

I looked at Steve, who'd lowered the glass I'd given him and wasn't smiling anymore.

"I knew it! You want to buy our house!"

Renee took the glass of water from Steve and said, "Avery, why don't you go start sorting the wood that came?"

"It's *my* house," I said. "I live there."

"Avery," Renee said, her voice sharp, and I fell silent.

"Steve, you should probably go now," she said, turning to him.

He nodded, then said, "Just think about it, all right? It would be a way for both of you to heal, to start to move on."

"I don't need to think about it," she said, and walked off toward the house. I watched Steve get into his car, all

smiles again, before I went after her. She was walking fast, angry fast, but I caught up to her.

"Does Steve want to buy my house?"

"Where are my drawings for the porch?"

"Renee, does Steve want to buy it?"

"Grandma," Renee said, her voice cracking. "You used to call me Grandma. We used to be a family. And now—" She shook her head, hard. "I feel like a stranger every time you say my name."

"Please answer my question," I said because I had to know. I had to hear it. I knew she was hurting, but I couldn't call her Grandma. I had lived with my parents until they'd been taken from me; I'd been part of a family that she hadn't been in for years and that history still lay between us.

"He wants to buy the house and your father's land," she said slowly.

"The house *and* the land? The forest Daddy loved, that Mom had her garden in? He wants all that?" My voice rose. "You don't get to decide that."

"I do, actually," Renee said. "You're seventeen, and I'm your guardian because we ... we're all the family that's left now."

"You ..." I said, shaking, and Renee grabbed my hands.

"I said no," she said. "Avery, I will never sell that land or the house."

"But you hate it," I whispered.

She flinched.

"I don't hate it, Avery. I live here too," she said. "The forest has . . . I do love it, but it's not as appealing to me as it was to your father. I can't be in it like your father was. I . . ." She trailed off, looking out into the trees, and then closed her eyes briefly, as if in pain.

She opened them and looked back at me. "I made a choice a long time ago, and I ended up with your grandfather and this life, and it gave me your father. I'll never be sorry for that. And no matter what the forest is or isn't to me now, I'd never sell your father's land. He loved the woods, Avery. Don't you think I know that?"

I looked at her. Her eyes were blue just like Dad's, and the expression in them, one of sadness, was one I'd seen in Dad's before.

He'd looked that way when he talked about Renee. About his mother, who he'd thought he'd lost because she didn't love him.

"You did love him," I whispered, and Renee said, "Oh, Avery, of course I did," and walked away again. I watched her go inside the kitchen, heard the sliding door shut. She sat at the kitchen table, looking out past me. Looking into the forest again.

I didn't follow her inside. I didn't look into the forest. I sat down on the lawn instead, the sun beating down on me, my mind spinning.

I'd just realized there was someone who understood exactly how lost and alone I felt.

And that someone was Renee.

My grandmother.

ten

"Do you want some more salad?" Renee asked as we ate dinner that night, and I shook my head, picking at the lettuce on my plate. The mushrooms in Renee's salad were strange, spongy and tasteless, nothing like the wild ones Mom had taught me to pick in the forest and that she always had on hand to sprinkle on things.

As much as I wanted to reach Renee, I couldn't because she wasn't Mom and Dad. She didn't know them, not like I did, and I knew she felt lost, I knew she missed them too, but she hadn't—

She didn't know what it was like to live with them. She'd lost her son and daughter-in-law. She hadn't lost everything. She hadn't lost her whole world.

"Let's start now," she said, pushing away her plate, and I blinked at her.

"The porch," she said. "We're not really eating dinner, are we?"

I looked at her plate. Her chicken had been cut into tiny pieces and her salad looked like mine, fork-pronged but basically untouched.

"Come on," she said, and her eyes . . . how had I never noticed exactly how much they looked like Dad's? The same hopefulness, the same expression of belief that things could change.

I'd never thought of Dad as getting anything from Renee, but that wasn't true at all.

"All right," I said, and got up. We went out the large sliding glass door in the kitchen, went out to where Renee's lawn stretched out toward the forest.

And then we dug holes.

I didn't think we'd do that. I thought you built something by hammering and nailing and stuff like that. I thought you put things on top of the ground.

"How's the porch going to stay in place if nothing's there to hold it?" Renee said when I said, "We have to dig holes?"

"There has to be support," she said. "So we put posts in, and then the wood is reinforced. Here, look at the drawings again."

I did. I didn't see any holes, but Renee gave me some weird-looking thing I recognized.

"Dad has one of these," I said, and remembered him outside putting on the last addition, the sunroom that was still in progress. He'd stood outside to plan it,

careful to go around the tree roots as he walked, and when he dug holes in the ground that I could see into, I saw that he'd left all the tree roots curled up safe and tight.

"Had," I said, my voice cracking as I realized Dad never would finish the sunroom. It would stay at the far end of the house, three walls and no ceiling. No paint, no wallpaper he or Mom found. No windows put in where Mom wanted windows to be.

"Don't hold it like that," Renee said and came over to me. She put her hands over mine and moved them around, down. "There you go." She took a deep breath.

"Your father liked doing this, you know. He dug the holes when I put in a fence."

"Fence?" I said, looking around. "You don't have a fence."

"Not now," she said. "I thought I'd try my hand at gardening one year, and that I'd better keep all the bunnies and such out. Got your father to dig the holes for the fence posts, and then he helped with the garden. Everything he planted grew and everything I did—well, he had a knack for it. Had this thing for pumpkins. Took one and fed it—"

"Milk," I said, my voice cracking a little. Dad had grown pumpkins every year and picked the biggest-growing one, cut a slit in the vine, and somehow gotten it to take in milk, the pumpkin always growing even more

enormous, so big that even after Mom canned it we ate pumpkin bread and pie for weeks.

"I never did grow much, but I loved that garden," Renee said. "I loved the idea of growing food. It made me feel closer to things. Push a little harder there, Avery. You actually need a hole deeper than a few inches."

"What things?" I said, but she motioned for me to keep digging.

I sighed, but did. I had no idea that digging holes was such hard work, but as Renee and I worked together, the silence between us got comfortable, not strange, and I watched her work, saw her carefully looking at the ground, making sure she didn't destroy anything where she dug.

She and Dad were so alike. I wished I'd seen it before now.

"How come you still live here?" I said.

"What do you mean?" Renee wiped one hand across her forehead. Her face was bright red, and she was breathing hard, but she'd dug up a lot more dirt than I had. She was stronger than she looked.

"You went really far away for a while, right?" I said. "But then you came back. Why?"

"I just did," she said, and then went back to digging, her mouth tight.

I looked at her, and she stopped digging again and looked at me.

"I wanted to come back," she said softly. "I wanted to be here. I used to tell your father that, and he . . . well, he never forgot that, although he forgot how much I wanted him to have a life that was bigger than mine."

"So Dad wanted to be like you? That's not bad. I don't understand why you two—"

"He could have been more," she said, her voice fierce. "He could have gotten a real job, had a career, but he stayed here working for that joke of a paper. I did the same thing, and what happened to me? I spent thirty years working for a dentist. I had a husband who . . ." She broke off.

"Who what?"

"Who was never happy here," she said, her voice quiet. "And it was hard on John. I wanted so much more for him."

"But he was happy," I said, and then realized that she wasn't. Not like she wanted to be, and that was why she had pushed Dad. Thirty years working for a dentist, and she hadn't loved it like Dad loved his job.

She hadn't loved my grandfather like Dad loved Mom. I'd heard that in her voice just now and it made me think of her house. How there were pictures of Dad and Mom and me in it, but none of her. None of my grandfather, who'd died back when Dad went to college.

"Were Dad and my grandfather . . . did they get along?"

"Of course," she said. "Why wouldn't they?"

"You don't have any pictures of him. And Dad never talked about him."

"I imagine he didn't talk about me either," Renee said, her voice quiet. "Gary was a good father."

She hadn't said he was a good husband.

"Were you—" I broke off, unsure of what to say. "Were you happy?"

"Of course," she said. "I wanted to be a wife and mother, to have a normal life. And I did. There's nothing wrong with that. With wanting to be like everyone else." Her voice rose a little on the last words, cracked like she wanted to believe them.

Wanted to, but didn't.

"What happened to the garden?" I asked.

"It never worked out like I wanted it to," she said and bowed her head, her mouth a sad, downward curve.

"I think we're done for the night," she said after a moment, and I didn't argue.

I thought we were too.

eleven

I didn't think I'd fall asleep but I did—digging holes was not only harder than it looked, but was tiring too— and when I woke up, I looked around for my alarm clock, the one Mom had actually bought me as a birthday present instead of finding it at a yard sale or something. It played ocean sounds that I liked to listen to when I was reading History. Anything—even History—read better if you could pretend you were by the ocean, the water breaking all around you.

But my alarm clock wasn't there. Had I dropped it? Knocked it off my nightstand?

I wasn't in my bed. My nightstand wasn't in the room. My clock wasn't in the room.

I'd thought I was at home, I really had, and I lay back down, pulling one of the two pillows on the bed close to me. I wasn't home. I was at Renee's. This was where I was supposed to be now.

But it wasn't where I wanted to be.

I hadn't been home since Ron found me. Since my parents were killed. I'd been given my clothes and some of my things, but I didn't have my alarm clock. I didn't have the crack in the wall that the wind whistled through, hot in the summer and cold in the winter.

I sighed into my pillow and then realized I could get up and leave.

I could go home.

The clock that wasn't my clock said it was just after one a.m. Renee would be asleep. I could go, slip out. Away.

I'd thought I understood longing. I'd read about it and even thought I'd felt it back when I wanted to have friends the first week or so I started at Woodlake High. I'd hoped for it, for friends, until I realized it wasn't going to happen.

But now I realized I hadn't understood longing at all. It wasn't about hope. It was about want, pure and simple.

I wanted to go home and Renee wouldn't stop me, not now. No one would.

I got up and got dressed. I slipped outside and into the forest.

I was wearing real clothes this time, jeans and a shirt Mom had given me, a simple but expensive shirt I'd seen in a magazine that had done a little article about her preserves.

"Don't tell your father," she'd whispered as she'd

given it to me, and I'd unfolded the soft, gray fabric and held it to my nose, smelling the scent of new. I'd loved it, of course, but I'd loved it even more once I slipped it on and found that the sleeves didn't just stop at the wrist. Instead there was fabric flowing free around them, like a flower blooming open around my hands.

It wasn't the best choice for the woods, though. Branches snagged me, my tired feet and legs sore from working with Renee and making me clumsy.

But I kept walking. I knew where I was going.

I was going home.

And then I was there, in the beginning of the woods I knew by heart, among the trees I'd sat by, alone or with Mom or Dad, and no branches caught me now because my feet knew where to go. I wove through the forest, stroking the bark of the first tree I'd ever climbed, and then paused to look at the tree Dad always sat and thought by.

"Daddy," I whispered, and above me tree branches creaked together. I didn't hear beauty in them. I didn't hear the world. But I did see Dad. Not like a hallucination, not like a dream. I remembered him, I saw him as he was, and I closed my eyes and imagined him here.

I imagined he was here with me.

"I'm thinking," he'd say, and then he'd smile, to show that he needed the time but still loved me, and I opened my eyes, rested my head against his tree. Wondered if it held all my father's thoughts.

"Do you know what happened?" I whispered to it, but the tree was silent, its branches falling still, hanging over me in the moonlight. It wasn't a full moon, but it was enough for me to see by and I started walking again, not hesitating at all. My parents had taught me how to move through the forest well.

And then I got to the house.

There was no longer any plastic on the ground but it was still disturbed, the soil turned over, broken. I even saw a few tree roots in the moonlight, the tiny, smallest stems peeking up. Brought out into the open by what had happened.

But there was no sign of my parents. No place that marked where their bodies had been. I told myself to remember.

Remember, I thought. *Remember.*

But I didn't. So I tried something different this time, just tried to keep my mind open and clear and not to think about that night, but nothing came.

My mind stayed silent, blank, and I just wanted to go inside the house.

So I did.

The front door was locked and had police tape across it but I knew where the spare key was kept, got it from the top of the front door, remembered Dad putting in a nail and showing me how I could reach it by standing on the footstool that was there to help us get our boots off in the winter.

I didn't need the stool now. I wasn't a little kid learning how to take off her boots or even how to get back to her home. I knew how.

And I knew I couldn't and wouldn't find mine, not really. Not like I wanted, with me and Mom and Dad all together. I knew I'd never find it for real.

I opened the door and slipped under the tape anyway.

The house smelled. I wanted it to smell like it always did, like food and Mom and Dad—like us—but it didn't. It smelled empty. Stale.

But I was still here, and it felt familiar in a way that nothing had since that awful night.

I wandered through the rooms. I went into the kitchen first. I looked at the dishes in the sink, the blue and red pottery plate Mom had traded preserves for back before they were selling for over thirty dollars a jar. I saw the glasses that didn't match and ran my fingers across them.

The fridge still worked—Dad had set up a solar cell that ran a generator when the power was turned off— and I could see our food. Our milk. Our juice. Dad's prunes in their little bag. The light flickered though, and I knew someone needed to check on the generator. Turn the solar panels so they got as much sun as possible. The house could run without electricity, but not like this. Not for so long.

I shut the fridge and went over to the kitchen table. I touched the napkins on it, the silverware. They all had

pieces of paper by them, police stuff, and yes, this was where we sat. Where we ate.

We'd had dinner, and then Mom had sent me out to get mushrooms. She'd had me do it before, of course, but she'd been so anxious about it that night, so clear that I had to go right then.

Why?

I looked at the napkins again, but there was no answer in them, and my own head stayed blank. Silent.

Tears burned my eyes. I wiped them away, then went into the living room. Dad's books—he was always reading at least five at a time—were still piled off to the side, and the labels Mom was making for the next round of canning were still on the coffee table. There were those little police notes around them again, around everything, but I didn't want to see them. I pretended them away.

It wasn't hard. I sat on the sofa and touched the spots where Mom and Dad sat, where we would watch the three channels we could get and Dad pretended he wasn't interested in who was going to win the latest season of the global travel reality show.

They'd left marks here, dips in the sofa, and I started to run my fingers over them but it wasn't the same. It wasn't them and I knew it.

Outside, I could pretend. Inside, it was quiet. Too quiet.

Inside, I knew they were gone all over again.

I didn't leave, though. I went into Mom and Dad's room next. I looked at their bed, at the rods Dad had built into the wall for their clothes. Mom's were hanging neatly on it. Dad's were mostly on the floor. That always drove Mom crazy. She'd always say, "You built the things, can't you put your clothes on them?"

I missed them fighting over stupid stuff like that. I touched the rods and wished.

I wished like I never had before, and nothing happened.

I went to my room last. My clock had gone dark, but I held it anyway, imagined it glowing like it used to, imagined that I had just woken up and was wondering what time it was. I looked out my window into the dark, into the forest, and lay back on my bed. It smelled like home.

Finally.

I was not going to cry and ruin that. I just picked up my pillow and held it close, let the scent of laundry detergent and fresh air from the clothesline wash over me, let the smell of the life I had fill me. Then I looked around my room, at the spaces where my things had been. They had been taken to Renee's but they belonged here. I belonged here.

I would stay. I would stay and live here. I could make it work. I'd figure out how to run the generator; I'd get the power turned back on somehow. I could ask the

Thantos family about it, maybe. I'd keep everything as it was.

I was home, and I wasn't going to leave.

And then I heard a noise. Faint, so faint, but real.

I knew my house, and what I heard wasn't the house. It was different. New.

I didn't think about being scared. I didn't think about anything other than that I was home and wanted to stay where I could still feel traces of my life, my parents.

I wanted that so badly it was all I could see, and so it was nothing to get up and walk toward the noise. What could be worse than what I'd lost?

I walked into the sunroom, into the room Dad had started but hadn't finished and I would do that, I would make the house whole.

When I walked into the sunroom, there was a shadow standing by the window, the one Dad had never put glass into. The window he was going to finish, but was killed before he could.

There was a shadow, and it . . .

The shadow was *it*, the thing that had taken my parents away from me.

I knew it. I didn't know how, but I did and *it* was there and it wanted . . .

I didn't know. I didn't remember. But if it wanted me, I was willing to go. Memories might be waiting for me. My parents would definitely be waiting for me.

So I stood there, staring at the shadow, and I wasn't afraid. I didn't shake. I didn't say anything.

I just waited for what was next.

And then the shadow moved.

It moved and I got scared. I didn't want to be, but I was. I took a step back.

"Avery," the shadow said, and its voice was sad. Familiar.

"Ben?" I said.

twelve

The shadow—Ben—said, "Yes."

I shook my head, surprised and a little embarrassed by what I'd thought, but he didn't explain why he was in my parents' home alone and this late at night. He didn't say anything.

He just stood there, staring at me.

And then he took a step forward.

"I told you the woods aren't safe for you," he said. "I can sen—feel it."

"You can *feel* it?" I said, and now I could see him. He'd moved into the place where the window was supposed to let light in and the moon shone, showed Ben looking at me, his dark hair gleaming, his lean body dressed, as usual, in simple jeans and a T-shirt, with moccasins once again on his feet.

He was beautiful.

Guys weren't beautiful. They were good-looking. Hot, Kirsta would have said about Ben, and I tried it out in my head a few times, but I couldn't say things like that and sound normal.

I wasn't normal. I'd spent sixteen years living in the woods.

But I knew, without a doubt, that Ben wasn't good-looking or hot. He was beautiful. His skin was pale, but not pale like pale should be. He didn't look sickly, or like he was from somewhere else. He didn't look other-worldly. He just looked like he was here and real and so, so gorgeous.

His skin shone. *He* shone, the moonlight catching his skin and falling off it, highlighting the perfection of his face. His cheekbones, high and sharp. His nose. Perfect too. His mouth—I looked at it and felt something cramp in my belly, heat snaking through me.

"You should probably go," he said, and his dark eyes stared into mine. I thought of Renee's house then, of the bed in the guest room that was my room now, and how it waited for me. I had to go to school when the sun rose, when another day began. It would be good to go home.

But Renee's house wasn't my home. This was, and I belonged here. Ben didn't.

"*You* should probably go," I echoed back. "This is my house, after all."

"You don't want to go back?" He sounded surprised.

"No, I don't," I said. "You can keep saying it, but you don't get to tell me what to do or where to go and you still haven't even said why you're here. You're in *my* house, and if you don't tell me why right now, I'm calling the police."

It was a lie. We had a phone, but if the house was running on what was left of the solar panels' charge, it meant the electricity was out. And that meant the phone—we had a line strung out here, one that was, as Dad said, "temperamental"—was gone too. The Thantos family had given up on having a phone years ago, as their part of the line was constantly falling down.

"You really aren't going?" Ben said, and he sounded so shocked that I said, "You do realize this isn't your house, right?"

"I know," he said, his voice solemn. "Avery, I came here tonight because I can fee—" He broke off.

"You can *feel*?" I said again.

"What happened here was terrible," Ben said as if he hadn't heard my question, as if he didn't want to talk about why he'd almost said "feel." "And it's not . . . Whoever did this isn't done. Not like they want. It isn't over, and you aren't safe. That's why I said you should go."

"And you feel all this how?" I said, and Ben looked away.

"I just . . . I just do, okay?" he said, and then stood straighter, like he was waiting for something.

To be told he was crazy, maybe. And maybe if he'd

told anyone else, they'd have said he was. But I'd grown up with parents who'd taught me that the world contained more than people saw, that there was possibility in everything. I lived in woods that no man had ever been able to reach the hidden heart of. I had sat with the torn-apart bodies of my parents, destroyed like they were nothing. Destroyed in way that a human couldn't—wouldn't—do. And I didn't remember it, or at least not enough to show me what had happened.

So why couldn't someone feel things? Sense that something awful had happened here? And if they could—

"Can you tell me who killed my parents?" I whispered. "Or do you—do you at least know why?"

He stared at me, his eyes widening slightly.

"You believe me?"

I nodded. "I've seen into the forest, way inside, back where people don't go. My mother loved to look at it, would sit outside and watch birds and look at the trees, look as far back as she could. And she let me look too. There's something there. Something old and strong, and people won't ever—there will always be woods here. Woodlake isn't—it's different. There is something stronger than humans here."

"You see that?"

"Yes," I whispered, caught by the awe in his voice as he stared at me.

"What else do you see?"

"Nothing," I said. "I don't remember what happened to my parents. I've tried so hard, but I can't see anything. I just . . . I saw blood. I remember feeling it soak into my shoes. My skin. And I saw silver shining, moving. Cutting. Moving like—moving like people can't."

"Silver? Like a weapon? A gun?"

"No. It was so fast, so silent, too silent to be a gun. And it was bright too. Brighter than any gun would be. What happened to my parents wasn't normal. Wasn't something a human could do."

"What?" he said, his voice very quiet, and off in the heart of the woods, a wolf cried out, a single, long call. A call that sounded like danger. A call that did not fear humans.

"I . . . maybe it was them," I said softly. "The wolves."

"Wolves?" Ben said, laughing, but the laughter came out strange. Harsh. Edged with fear. "Wolves don't attack people."

I took a deep breath. "Not usually. Not regular ones. But there are stories about ones who are more than wolves and who live in the woods. Who look like people but aren't human and can—"

"Stories?" he said. "Did your parents tell you this?"

"No," I said. "My father said it was all stuff people made up a long time ago."

"So why do you believe it? I mean, it sounds . . . well, crazy."

"Just because you haven't seen something doesn't mean it can't be real," I said. "I can't remember what happened, but I remember seeing their bodies when I looked back as Ron was driving me away, and they—they were torn apart."

My voice broke, but I kept going. "What happened to them wasn't—people don't do that. Can't do that. And I saw that silver, and it was so different. Inhuman. Silent, and that's the thing. People make noise. But a wolf that's more than a wolf wouldn't."

"Even if there was something like that and even if . . ." His voice cracked. "Even if that could happen, why would someone like that kill your parents?"

"The forest is shrinking. Its outer edges are gone. You said you could sense the want that someone has for this place. And if you had nowhere else to go, and people were in your way—" I broke off, my voice catching on a sob. If only my rotten, blocked head would work. Would *see*.

"That wouldn't happen. Couldn't happen," he said, and reached for me. His arms were strong and warm and comforting. "And Avery, there's no trace of animals here from what happened. Just blood. Just humans."

"My parents," I said. "Are they still—can you feel them here?"

"No. I'm sorry. I know you must miss them, but I just know something terrible happened here. Something that isn't over. But I'll look out for you."

I looked up at him, so close, and he looked back at me. His mouth parted and he touched my face, the fingers of one hand, one long, pale hand, sliding across my cheek, his thumb catching on my lower lip.

"Avery," he said, "I can't—"

And then he kissed me.

I could actually feel him struggling against it—the kiss, and me—how he stiffened right before his lips met mine. And then how he gave in, and the way his mouth met mine.

He kissed me like I was the only girl in the entire world, like he had to kiss me. Like he couldn't stop himself. He kissed me like I was someone special, like he—like he cared about me.

He kissed me like he wanted me.

And I wanted him.

I forgot everything—where I was, how I'd found him in the house, what he'd said, my worry, my fear—all of it. What he felt—his want—flowed into me, filled me, and I saw I was beautiful.

Me, plain Avery, was beautiful to Ben. And he'd wanted—

Oh. I felt how much he'd craved a touch and more—this—since he first saw me. Since that first day at school when I'd seen him and thought he'd barely noticed me.

"Avery," he panted, pulling away. "I can feel your emotions, and you can—"

"Yes," I said, "*yes*," and I didn't know what I was saying, I just wanted him to kiss me again. I wanted him and he pulled me close and we pushed against each other, his arms wrapping around my waist, then lower, pulling me against him, and I went, I pushed closer still, as close as I could, and we ended up slowly sinking to the floor, still kissing, our hands starting to touch each other, brief caresses across the back of the neck. The shoulder. Down the arm.

He shivered when I touched him, and I—

I melted when he touched me.

I had never been kissed before. I never even knew a kiss could be like this, never knew that being with someone could be like this, but now I understood why you could want someone so much you'd forget everything because it felt better than good. It was like the sun bursting open inside me and he pushed his hips against mine and I pushed back, aching, drawing him closer, hearing him breathe hard as he kissed my neck and then came back to my lips.

His hand shook as it slid under my shirt, and I arched up, wanting his touch, wanting him, and ran my own hands down his sides, feeling the warmth of his skin through his shirt and then slipping under it.

His skin was soft, but I could feel the muscles beneath it, the ridge of his stomach, the strong line of his back. He groaned and now I shivered. His fingers traced the

bottom of my bra, and I needed him to touch me, I needed his hands on me, I wanted everything, I craved—

My hand slid up his back, touched his shoulder blades. He stiffened, gasped, "Avery," his voice cracking.

But it was too late.

My fingers rolled down into the notch between his shoulder blades, ready to trace the skin on his spine, ready to pull him closer, to get him to touch me more. Forever.

Between his shoulder blades I felt a tiny patch of hair, a small triangle about two fingers wide. Downy soft, like baby's hair, impossibly soft. But it was hair. Not baby's hair, but something else.

Not human hair. And the shape of it, the pattern—

I drew my hand away, shocked, and he pushed up, his face contorted, his mouth open like he was in pain.

"Avery," he whispered, and I looked at my hand.

Saw the hairs clinging to it.

Short hairs, like an animal would shed.

Silver hairs, like a wolf had.

I scrambled back, pushing away from his hands, but I was still sitting down, I was still on the floor and he was close and what—?

What was he?

"It's not what you're thinking," he said, like he knew what I felt, and I knew—

I knew, right then, that he did know. Not just because he'd told me so, but because I'd felt his emotions, the whole tumbled mess of them, when he'd touched me.

"It's this weird skin thing and I'm going to get it removed as soon as I save enough money for it," he said. "That's all it is."

I could sense the desperation coming off him. The fear. The lie.

"No," I said. "It's not—this isn't a weird skin thing at all. It's something that . . . it's something that only comes out when you—*when you've been something else.*"

He stared at me, and I stared right back.

He looked away first, but not before I glimpsed his eyes flashing, the color seeming to shift to silver.

"Avery—I—"

And then he stopped. Closed his eyes, breathing like he was in pain, and I swear he rippled for a moment, his whole body shuddering like something was underneath it. Inside it.

"You should go," he whispered, and somehow I managed to stand up, never turning away from him. I'd thought I'd needed him and now—

"I won't hurt you," he said. "I'd never hurt you."

I ran then.

I ran because I was scared.

I ran because I knew that he was scared.

I ran because I didn't know if he was telling the truth, and because he didn't either.

I ran through the woods. I wasn't careful this time. I didn't stop at the places my parents loved. I wanted out; I wanted to be at Renee's.

I wanted none of this to be real even as the memory of his mouth on mine, his hands on my skin, made me burn.

Made me want him even though—

I stumbled across a tree root, almost falling, and off in the distance, there was a cry. A wolf cry.

No, I told myself. *No.* But I didn't believe it like I wanted to.

I was so close to Renee's backyard, to safety, and I kept going, my hands pushing branches away, the moonlight catching on tiny silver strands of hair.

The stories I'd heard from Kirsta said there were wolves who could walk among us. That when the town was founded, those wolves who were more than wolves had wanted human women. And had gotten them.

The town had sent girls to men who lived deep in the forest, to men who looked like everyone else. But who weren't like them at all.

Ben hadn't even told me why he was really at my parents' home. He'd sensed something, danger, and told me to be careful but—

What if he'd meant himself?

I stumbled into the house, barely managing to stay quiet, and went back to the guest room.

I lay on the bed, remembering what happened. It had been so frightening to see Ben in my home, and then he'd made me—

No. He hadn't made me want him. He had been as

drawn to me as I was to him. I knew he'd tried to get me to go home, remembered I'd thought about doing that for just a moment before I'd pushed it away. He'd seemed so surprised by that.

I remembered how he'd kissed me.

How I kissed him back.

How I—

I rolled onto my side. There was still one—just one—small silver hair on my hand. Clinging still, as if to remind me of what had happened. What I'd done.

I was terrified, and not just because I was afraid I knew what Ben was. I was terrified because I remembered his kiss, his touch—and I craved it again.

I wanted him.

thirteen

I woke up exhausted. I hadn't slept much, and when I had, I'd dreamed of Ben, of what had happened between us, and then things had changed and it happened again, but now his back was smooth and he smiled at me and said, "I'm fine now. I can control it, Avery, I swear," and I reached for him and—

And he shuddered in my arms, growled my name into my ear, and I looked at him and saw silver, saw—

I jerked awake with a start.

My mind wouldn't even let me think the word, much less about what I'd just dreamed.

"Avery," Renee said, and I sat up too fast, making myself dizzy.

"Why are you still in bed?"

"I don't feel so good."

She came over and touched my forehead.

I knew she felt it when I stiffened, and I wanted to tell her it wasn't her, it was my thoughts, but I knew she wouldn't believe me.

"No fever," she said, her voice quiet.

I tried anyway. "Renee, when you were checking to see if I was sick, I wasn't—"

"It doesn't matter," she said sadly, and then, "I hope we can get to know each other again. I hope that you . . . that you want to."

"I do," I said, and realized I meant it. Not just because she was all I had left in the world, or because I could see Dad in her, but because she was my grandmother and I had loved her so much when I was young, and love can be broken but never forgotten.

Mom used to say that to Dad. I'd always wondered why she had when they were so happy.

I was pretty sure I knew why now, and I looked at Renee. She and my dad had been broken, but now I wondered if Renee herself had somehow been broken too.

"I'm going to go make you some breakfast," she said, standing up, her voice brisk as she looked away from my gaze. "Do you feel well enough to go to school?"

"I'm fine," I said, and so I got up and went.

I only had one class with Ben, and it was the last class of the day. I'd get through it. It was only one class.

Or I could just transfer out. I'd be able to do that,

I was pretty sure, and then I'd get away from him and that would be it. Problem solved.

Except I kept thinking about him.

And then I saw him the moment I walked into school.

I blinked, sure I was dreaming, but no, he was there, standing by a locker as a girl talked at him. She was smiling, trying to get him to look at her, but he didn't notice her at all.

I knew because he wasn't looking at her.

He was looking at me.

He was looking at me, but then he just turned around and walked off. The girl who'd been trying to talk to him acted like everything was fine, and even called out, "Bye, Ben! See you later," but I watched people shoot her looks.

Their gazes swam right over me.

He'd turned away from me. *I* was going to avoid *him* and instead he looked at me and then just left. Like we hadn't kissed, like last night he hadn't been touching me, wanting me.

I stopped in the hall, stunned. After what I'd seen, after everything, I was—

I was hurt.

Someone bumped me and I moved to the side, got bumped again, and heard, "Avery?"

I looked over and saw Kirsta.

"Hey," she said. "Are you heading to first period?"

I nodded, waiting for her to do something like yell

that I was cursed again, but instead she said, "Avery, I'm sorry, okay?"

I looked at her. We'd started walking down the hall and no one was looking at me at all, just like how things used to be, and no one was looking at her either.

Now I knew why she was talking to me again.

"No one wants to hear you talk about me anymore," I said.

She turned bright red. "I didn't mean...I just wanted—"

"I know," I said, because I did. "You wanted it to be like it was for you before."

"I just—people wanted to talk to me, Avery. I mattered, you know? I want people to see me like they used to." She sighed. "But it didn't last at all, and I don't think you're cursed. You just streaked your hair or whatever, and I..." She trailed off. "I really am sorry."

I nodded and she smiled.

"Just like that? It's okay?"

"Kirsta, people have talked about me since I first came here," I said. "I guess I'm used to it."

"Well, I have a plan. I heard something this morning that is completely mind-blowing, and I'm going to hint that I heard it to Jackie later, and you know how she is. If I can get her to talk to me, then everyone else..." She kept talking, but I stopped listening.

I didn't exactly know who Jackie was. I was pretty sure

she was one of the four girls Kirsta said ruled the school, and that I'd seen her, watched her make plans to do things I didn't care about at all. I didn't want to drive for hours and try on clothes inside a mall that faked light, that had no fresh air.

But Kirsta needed that, wanted that; she craved the ability to walk around school and have people know who she was. To like her, or at least say they did. I might not know exactly who Jackie was, but I'd heard how great and how awful she was in the same sentence by more than one person.

I didn't want what Kirsta did. I'd hoped high school would be fun, that maybe I'd find people I could talk to, but Kirsta needed to count to everyone and I just didn't see the point in it. I never had, and now I really didn't.

Kirsta's world wasn't my world. My world was the forest. My world was my parents, and I wanted to know what had happened to them. I wanted to know why it had.

And I wanted to know who—or what—did it.

"Avery?" Kirsta said and I blinked, realized we were standing right where we usually said good-bye as the two of us each headed off to our classes.

"I was just...good luck," I said to her and she said, "Thanks," and smiled at me. It was a small one, a shaky one.

She knew we had nothing in common. She'd known it for longer than I had, I realized, but she'd still talked to me. She'd talked to me until my parents had died and I had changed.

"See you around?" she said, and I wished I was that girl again, the one who didn't belong but could at least try and live in this world with its hallways and gossip. But I wasn't, and couldn't. It all seemed like shadows to me now. Like nothing.

"Kirsta," I said, but she shook her head, said, "You don't care about any of this, do you?"

"Not really."

"I wish I was like you," she said. "Everyone knew who you were even before your parents died. You're just you, and you're okay with that. You could have been so popular but you never—you never even noticed that it was just there, waiting for you. You talked to me instead."

"I wasn't—" I had no idea what she was saying. Me, popular? No one had ever noticed me here. I was a nobody until my parents died, and now I was a weird nobody. "That's not how it was at all."

"Why do you think I talked to you in the first place? I thought I could come with you. But you never wanted to be popular at all and you never will, will you?"

"No," I said, and Kirsta's sad smile got sadder.

"I was a shitty friend. I'm sorry for that too," she said.

The bell rang then and she was gone, swept up in the crowd heading toward classes.

I sat through first period wondering about what she'd said. I didn't believe most of it, but I did feel like everything had changed. The scary thing was I had no idea what was going to happen next.

I glimpsed Ben in the hallway again right after class, like I'd called him somehow, and he started to come toward me.

Then he stopped and turned away.

As he did, his eyes flashed, and they flashed silver.

fourteen

I told myself to get out of school then. Get Renee to come get me. Go talk to Ron.

But what could I say to him? "I met the new guy, Ben, and his eyes sometimes look silver and I don't think he's human. Oh, and I also made out with him and can't stop thinking about it."

Ron would have been nice, but he would have patted me on the head and sent me home, or to a mental institution. Eyes that I believed looked silver? It was like something out of a story, and no one had been with me when any of what I'd seen or felt with Ben had happened.

I also didn't want to tell anyone about him. Ben had been worried about me before, and last night he'd kept telling me to be careful. If he'd killed my parents, why would he do that? My death would mean I'd never remember, that whatever—and even now, I couldn't think of Ben as an *it*, I just couldn't—killed them would never be caught because the one person who saw it was gone.

And he'd said my name like I was someone special. He'd looked at me like he had to.

He'd looked at me like he couldn't look away, and I knew that last night had happened in spite of himself, that he'd been trying to stay away from me . . . and that he couldn't.

I remembered him saying my name and then the feel of his mouth on mine, and for once I couldn't get myself to care about what I was supposed to be learning, couldn't even get myself to focus. My thoughts were somewhere else. With someone else.

In English class, we had to go to the library. We were supposed to be doing research on Milton and *Paradise Lost* for our term project papers. I sat down to search the databases the librarian had left open for us on every computer, but ended up ignoring them and looked for something else.

Woodlake didn't have enough money to put decent filters on their school computers, so it was easy enough to get off the databases and into a search engine. I typed in "wolves" and "Woodlake," my hands sweating.

There were a lot of matches, but one was . . .

One made my skin prickle as I read the little blurb under it.

I was sure it wouldn't turn out to be anything, and then I clicked on the link, read a page on a website about shape-shifters. The story it told was one I knew already, the story of how Woodlake was founded. How people came through the great forest long ago, and found that the soil was rich and wished to stay. How they began to cut down the forest.

How the settlers began to die.

And then two men who weren't men at all came out of the woods and told the settlers to leave one tree standing in the town, a reminder of the forest and all that it stood for. They'd also asked for wives, and two girls were sent into the woods to become the brides of men who were more than just men.

Someone had drawn a picture illustrating that moment, two girls in old-fashioned clothing standing together under a tree, their hands clasped together like they were holding each other up. It looked like a made-up picture, like something from a fairy tale, except for one thing.

The tree the girls stood by was the one that stood in the center of town. The one Dad had loved so much, the one that seemed to watch over all of Woodlake, spreading up high into the sky, over the tallest building, over the tops of the newest homes that had been built, homes that had started to eat away part of the forest.

The last sentences read: "Although no sightings have

ever been officially reported, Woodlake still remains a small community surrounded almost entirely by a forest where wolf cries can be heard almost every night. It is rumored that certain extinct wolves, like the *Dusicyon australis*, live there, and also rumored that the wolf cries sometimes sound more human than animal."

Dusicyon australis.

Ben Dusic.

My hands shook as I typed "Dusicyon australis."

They shook more as I found something.

Something about wolves.

There had once been wolves classified with a scientific name that started with Dusic. They had never been anywhere near Woodlake. They were extinct, and had been for a long time.

Or at least, they were supposed to be.

Ben had lost his family recently, just like I had. He had just moved here from somewhere called Little Falls. I didn't know where that was, and I bet no one did. He was living with his great-uncle, Louis. I knew who he was.

I closed the windows I had opened on the computer, and thought about one more search I could do.

One more word, the name given to those who were part wolf, part man. A name used in stories I'd read, stories everyone had heard. Stories that my father had been so quick to tell me weren't true.

I didn't search. I already knew what Ben was.

Dusicyon australis.

Wolf.

I didn't want to believe it, but it all fit. I lived in a small town, a town that was surrounded by forest. Lots of towns had forests around them, but not many had forests like Woodlake's.

But Woodlake's forest was slowly starting to shrink as more people moved here. Soon we'd probably have strip malls and coffee shops. Eventually, places like the Thantos house—like my house, homes that lay surrounded by the forest—would all be gone. Maybe one day no one would live in the woods, but I had and I couldn't forget my life there. I wouldn't.

I also couldn't forget what had happened when I was with Ben.

Or what I'd read just now.

I should have left school, if only to clear my head, but I didn't, and I knew why the second I walked into Art.

Ben.

I walked over to my easel. I had to walk past him, and as I did he stared straight ahead, a muscle in his jaw jumping.

"I know where 'Dusic' comes from. What it means," I whispered.

He flinched, then stilled. "It's just a name. It's—" He stopped as he saw the look on my face, turned so he was facing his easel and not me. "Look, I just moved here. I'm

just trying to get used to the town. To everything. And you . . ." He trailed off.

"I know what you are," I said, and he looked at me then.

"I know you do," he said.

It wasn't what I had expected him to say, and I stared at him, shocked. "You do?"

"I felt it when you realized it last night," he said. "When you believed it today. I feel your emotions, Avery. The strong ones, the deep ones. And you feel mine. And that . . . it shouldn't be happening. But I can't stop it."

"I'm not like you," I said, my voice shaking. "I'm a person, not a—not what you are, and I don't sense emotions. That's not possible. You can see how people feel, but you can't *know* how they feel."

He looked at me and I remembered how I'd felt last night. How I'd somehow known what he wanted. I was all he could think about, all he was thinking about, even now, and he ached to kiss me again. He didn't care who saw; he just wanted last night to happen again and again and again.

Forever.

I burned to turn toward him, to take just that breath of movement that was needed to confirm what we both knew was true, that the heat that beat between us was bigger than both of us.

We could be something amazing—or we could end up destroying each other.

I couldn't let that happen. I had to know what

happened to my parents. I couldn't let them have died because of the whim of something so full of brutality that there were no words for the monsters in its soul. For something that wanted the forest for a reason even Ben hadn't been able to understand, that went so deep and angry it was as if it had no end.

So I moved, but not toward Ben.

I walked to the other side of the room. I stood near Kirsta. She glanced at me as I set up my easel, noticed my shaking hands.

She didn't say anything. She helped me set up, and I wished I could talk to her. She had told me the story Dad had worked so hard to convince me was false. She might understand.

But she wouldn't. I knew it. And Ben knew it too.

Even away from him, even across the room, I could still feel his thoughts because they were so strong. So full of want.

I could feel my face turning red, and I stared at the forever dying apples we were still drawing.

It was the longest class of my life, and when the bell finally rang, I ran out of the room as fast as I could. I didn't stop, even though people were looking at me.

I ran because if I had hesitated for even a second when class ended, I would have gone to Ben. In spite of what I knew, in spite of what little memory I had of that night—*silver*—it was all nothing compared to how he made me feel.

My heart said Ben was Ben in spite of everything I'd learned today, but then my heart had also believed my parents would be around forever.

I didn't think I could trust myself, and so I ran outside, ignoring my locker, homework—all the things that were supposed to be my life—and looked for Renee's car.

I didn't see it, so I kept running down the sidewalk, looking.

And then I ran right into Louis, Ben's great-uncle.

fifteen

A very," he said as I bounced—and I did bounce, he was all muscle even though his face was lined and his hair was white—off him. "I was sorry to hear about your parents."

"Thank you," I said automatically even as I stared at him. He was Ben's great-uncle. Was he like Ben?

"You've met my nephew," he said, his voice very soft. "And I can see that you've seen something in him that most people wouldn't have. But it isn't what you think. Ben is just like you. Think about it and you'll see." His voice was still very soft, very soothing. I could almost feel it pulling at me, as if by saying something Louis could make me believe it was true. "Remember, Ben is just like you, just like everyone else."

"No, he's not," I said, and Louis blinked at me. He had dark brown eyes but there were streaks of another color in them. Silver.

I shivered because now I knew for sure exactly what he was too.

"You're like Ben, aren't you?"

"Well," Louis said, staring at me. "Ben said that if I spoke to you like I would to anyone else, you wouldn't listen. You do have a heart and mind that stay clear no matter what you hear, don't you?"

"You didn't answer my question."

"Do I need to?"

I looked at him.

"No," I finally said.

Louis smiled. He had even, white teeth. Not threatening, but there was something not quite human about them. About him.

"You're Ben's only family?" I said.

"Yes, now," Louis said. "There are . . . there are dangers for those like us. Ben's father tried to avoid them, but he was unable to."

"And is there danger here?"

"Not like he saw, and hopefully not ever," Louis said. "I don't think we need to talk about this anymore."

"Fine. How about you tell me who killed my parents?"

"Something evil," he said after a moment. "That's what it is, and that's the traces it's left behind. Whatever killed your parents wants the woods, but not to keep. To destroy."

"But it's not after you?"

"No."

"Could you find what killed my parents and stop it?"

Louis shook his head slowly. "I'm old, and I've lived alone for too long. The world has passed me by in many ways, and I chose that. But now I cannot stop whatever wants the forest. It is something I do not understand. But you—Avery, you can stop it, and that is why you must be careful. You understand the woods in a way that is rare. You see them for what they are and they see you. You have power, and evil always wants that."

"Power?" I didn't laugh, but I wanted to. I was seventeen, my parents were dead, and my life was—I had just spent my last class trying not to go to Ben, who was part wolf. I had no power. I had no memory of who killed my parents and longed for someone who belonged in a myth. Who wasn't supposed to be real.

"Yes, power," Louis said. "Once, many years ago, there was someone like you, but she did not want—I must stop. Ben is coming this way."

"Hold on. If I have power, what is it? And why didn't it work when my parents were dying?"

"I don't know. The forest is home to me, but it doesn't open its heart. I only know that in Woodlake the woods have ties to something older than anything that has ever lived here, and that it is in you."

"That doesn't tell me anything."

"I'm sorry," Louis said. "Who you are and who you will

be is something you will have to decide, and sooner rather than later, I think. But Ben must not—he must not be hurt. You cannot let him die for you."

"He wouldn't," I said, shocked, and Louis looked at me.

"He would," he said. "I do not ask for favors often, but I must ask you for one now. Let Ben go. Turn your emotions from him."

"Wait a minute. I didn't ask for this," I said. "He talked to me, he—"

"It isn't fair, I know," Louis said. "But you saw something truly evil and I cannot lose Ben to it. "

Louis wasn't making me feel very secure about my future. "So you want me to not think about Ben and, by the way, you know something wants to kill me but you have no idea what?"

"I'm sorry I can't help more, but letting Ben go will not be as hard as you think. Humans forget—" He swallowed. "They forget more easily than others."

I stared at him. "You said there was someone like me. Who was she? What happened to her? Did she die?"

"No, she chose to forget what she'd seen. What she was." His voice was full of pain.

"Avery?" Ben said from behind me, and then, "Louis?" his voice lower, angrier. "She's upset. What did you say to her?"

"Only the truth," Louis said. "We have to go."

"But—"

"Ben," Louis said, and I heard the pleading in his voice. The love. The fear.

I knew what it was like to lose someone you loved, and Louis loved Ben. I couldn't feel it, but I could feel Ben's confusion and his worry.

Louis was all the family Ben had left, and the last thing I wanted was more blood on my hands.

And if it was Ben's—

If it was Ben's, I couldn't bear it.

"I have to go," I said, and walked away. I tried to keep my mind blank. To not feel anything for Ben.

"Avery," Renee called, and I went to her.

"Who were you talking to?" she said.

"A neighbor. He lived near us. Not down by the Thantos family, but out in the other direction. Louis Dusic."

"Oh. And he wanted—?" Renee's voice was strange. Strained.

"To say he was sorry about Mom and Dad. You've talked to him, right? Is he always so . . . intense?"

"Everyone knows everyone around here," Renee said, an answer that wasn't really one at all. "Are you ready to go?"

"We should work on the porch," I said on the way to her house, and made myself think about it, forcing myself to think of wood and nails and not Ben.

"I suppose there are a few things we could do before dinner," Renee said. She slowed down as we got near her

mailbox at the end of her driveway. She rolled down her window and waved at the car—the police car—that was sitting on the side of the road across from her house.

"Ron," she said, "what are you doing here? Is there news?"

Ron nodded, and then looked at me.

"I'm sorry," he said.

My heart sank.

"All right, you'd best come inside," Renee said. Her mouth was tight and sad as we pulled into her driveway.

Ron followed, getting out of his car as we did, and Renee looked at him and then said, "I'll fix us something to drink in the kitchen," her voice too cheerful, all brittle edges.

Ron nodded, looking uncomfortable.

"How are you?" he asked me. "Feeling all right? Any new memories I should know about?"

There are wolves in the woods, Ron. Wolves that are more than wolves, that are part human, and I'm supposedly bound to one and can feel his most intense emotions. Oh, and something definitely wants me dead, but no one knows what.

"No," I said, "not a thing," and we all went inside.

sixteen

I'll get right to it," Ron said as we were all sitting at the
kitchen table, nodding at me as I handed him a glass of
lemonade that Renee had made and put into a pitcher.
"All the tests I've had done have come back with nothing
to help us identify who killed and mutilated—" He
cleared his throat, glancing at me.

Mutilated. That was what had been done to my parents. I'd seen them lying broken under plastic, I'd seen
what had been done to them, and even if I couldn't remember the during in spite of all my attempts, each one more
frustrating than the last, I did remember the after. How
I'd screamed. And to hear what had happened to them all
over again now, in Renee's sunny afternoon kitchen as I
held a glass of lemonade . . .

I thought of how I'd walked through my home last
night, of how everything was the same and yet there were

already signs that the house was fading. That what it had held—my life—was fading.

"Avery," Renee said gently, putting her hands on my wrist. Her fingers were warm. I blinked and unclenched my hand from around my glass, carefully setting it down as Renee glared at Ron.

"I shouldn't have said those things. I'm sorry," Ron said. "I cared about John and Debby and I—" He broke off and set his own glass down, placing his palms flat on the table. "I never expected to see something like this happening in Woodlake, and to have it happen to such good people, it really makes you wonder about what's out there. It makes you think about the evil in this world."

"You watch over all of us. That counts for more than enough," Renee said. "But how can nothing have turned up?" Her face was pale as she said it, and I could tell she didn't like hearing what Ron had said about the test results any more than I did.

"I don't know," Ron said, his voice grim. "You know, I'd like to see Woodlake grow, though not at the rate Steve wants, but with what happened and how there's no trace at all, well, it's a little frightening. It reminds me of the stories people used to tell when John and I were kids, the ones about how Woodlake managed to become a town and how—"

"No," Renee said, and pushed away from the table. "I am not going to listen to a bunch of nonsense about

the forest. You can't find anything, so you come out here with a story, Ron? Really? You truly believe that some storybook creature killed my son and my daughter-in-law?"

"You've lived here your whole life, Renee," Ron said. "You've heard all those wolf cries, and you know as well as I that sometimes they don't sound like wolves at all. I know John never believed in it at all, but you must know that sometimes they sound—"

"Stop," I said, and Renee and Ron both looked at me.

"Avery?" Ron said, and came over to me, knelt down. "Did I say something that—are you remembering something? You've gone so pale, and—Renee—look, her pupils are dilated." He lowered his voice. "What is it? What do you see or remember? Anything that's come to you, anything at all would be so much help. You're the only one who can help now, in fact. Tell me what you know. What you saw."

Ben, I thought, and remembered being with him, forgetting everything but him, and then feeling his back, that tiny pattern on it, and realizing he wasn't just a guy. That he belonged to the woods in a way I never, ever would.

"I went to the house," I whispered, and Renee let out a little cry, leaned back against the kitchen counter like it was the only thing holding her up. "I wanted to go home."

"When?" Ron said.

"I—a while ago," I said.

"Why would you do that?" Ron said, sighing. He took off his hat and ran a hand through his hair. "It's still a crime scene. It's not safe."

I looked at the floor, not wanting to say more. I could tell I'd upset Ron, who'd been the one to box up all my things and bring them to Renee's, who'd seen how scared I was in the hospital and sat with me for hours while I talked to what seemed like hundreds of people, who'd said, "It's enough; let her rest," when they pushed, frustrated by my empty memories.

"She went out a few nights ago," Renee said softly. "Avery, why didn't you tell me where you'd gone?"

I remembered Ben telling me to be careful in the forest, and then I thought of Louis, telling me today that I had some sort of power, and that evil always wanted power.

I shrugged, feeling a shiver crawl up my spine.

"I can't believe this," Ron said, his voice full of sorrow. "You went out there all by yourself? You should have let your grandmother take you. I would have taken you if you'd just called me. But you can't take any risks now. Not when we have no way to find out who killed your parents. You haven't been out there again, have you?"

I shook my head because I hadn't. And because I didn't want to talk about it anymore, didn't want to think about what I'd seen.

Who I'd seen.

"Renee," Ron said, standing up and turning to her. "In light of everything and how Avery is—well—" He motioned for her to move toward him, and then said something so low-voiced I couldn't hear it.

I didn't need to, though, because Renee said, "The house? The town council wants to tear it down? But how can they do that? It's John's land, not town land. Is Steve behind this?"

"I know how it sounds, I do," Ron said. "But without John around to take care of the house, which wasn't in the best shape to begin with—you know how he was, and Renee, there's worry that it's just going to fall apart and maybe hurt someone. Plus with the murders still so fresh in everyone's minds, there's also just a lot of fear. And yes, Steve did speak out for it."

"No," I said, standing up, shaking. "Not the house! It's mine, it's all I have left! Renee, you can't let them—"

"It's not about taking the house away from you," Ron said, looking at me. "The town council can rule that a building is unsafe, and it is. I'll make sure I know the guys who take it down, all right? Whatever you want, I'll make sure they get it for you."

He looked back at Renee. "This isn't what I wanted to tell you. You know that. And with all this happening, I don't want you suffering more. Without the house, you'll just be paying taxes on land that . . ." He sighed. "It hurts me to think about what's happened, so I know how it must

hurt you too. I know Steve came out here, and I know he comes across as—well, Steve, but I do think he means well, and if selling means Avery can go to college without worrying about money, then maybe it is worth thinking about."

"No," Renee said, pushing away from the counter. "You tell the town council they can knock the house down, and you tell Steve I am not selling him one single thing. My son loved the forest, and ripping it away and putting up a plaque or something with his name on it—that's exactly what Steve would do, and John would never forgive me for that. I could never forgive *myself* for that."

"John would want Avery taken care of."

"I'll take care of Avery," Renee said. "And I'll respect my son and what he would have wanted. It's all I can do now, Ron."

"Are you sure? I don't want guilt to make you feel like you have to do things," Ron said, but Renee shook her head.

"It's not guilt," she said. "It's love. I wish you'd stopped by with better news, though."

Ron nodded and picked up his hat. "I do too," he said quietly.

"I know," Renee said, patting his shoulder.

When he was gone, she looked at me. "Avery, I hope you understand. Even if the house is gone, that land is—"

"Daddy would be happy to know the land is safe," I said. "Mom too. Thank you."

She nodded, her eyes bright. "You shouldn't go out there again, though. At least not alone. All right? Your father was good at building things but—"

"I know," I said, thinking of the crack in my bedroom wall. Of the sunroom that had never been finished.

Thinking of all that I'd had, and how it was gone forever now.

seventeen

Ben wasn't in school the next day. It was good that he wasn't. I needed to think, and when he was around, I was distracted. Not focused, and definitely not thinking of ways to save my home.

Not that him being gone really helped with any of it. I found myself wondering where he was. What he was doing. If he was okay.

I was starting to think that what Ben and Louis had said was real, that between Ben and me was something that drew us to each other and let us sense each other's strongest feelings. As I sat in class, trying to think of ways to appeal to the town council and coming up blank, maybe Ben could really feel my frustration, my worry.

And then I . . .

I *felt* something. I felt like Ben was there, inside my head. I knew, somehow, that he could tell I was upset, and that he was worried about me.

This can't be, I thought, and what I got in return was the same surprise. The same sense that this—us—shouldn't be, but yet it was.

I went to the library at lunch, and looked up mind-reading online instead of eating. All I found was lots of pages containing stories about people who could supposedly pass every thought they had to someone else. Sometimes they could even see what the other person was doing.

That wasn't what was happening to me. I couldn't read Ben's mind and he couldn't read mine. I couldn't somehow see what he was doing. I just knew that when I felt something strongly—painfully or otherwise—he somehow felt it too. And I felt the same from him.

But that wasn't mind reading. I was confused now—worried, actually—but when I thought of Ben, he wasn't there anymore.

I'd sensed his worry for me all morning, had felt his feelings become a strangely reassuring presence in my head because knowing someone was thinking about me made me feel less alone.

Now that it was gone, I wondered about wolves, Ben, and what I knew.

And yet I wasn't scared. Not of him, anyway.

I was scared of me. I knew what Ben was—that he was more than human—and it didn't scare me. It didn't make me want to run and tell someone. It didn't make me want to hide.

It didn't make me want to stay away from him.

I got through Art without Ben by making myself sketch what I did remember about my parents. It was a long shot, and I knew it, but nothing else had worked, so why not try and see if my hands could pull something out of my mind? What if I could draw what I had seen but yet couldn't see at all?

The teacher came by, saw my page, all blood red with flashes of silver off to the side, almost out of sight, and cleared her throat.

But she knew what had happened to my parents too, of course, and just said, "You don't need to turn that in," sending me a soft look of pity before she turned away.

That was it. That was what I needed to save the house.

Pity.

I could go to the next town council meeting and talk about how I'd lost everything and couldn't even remember it. How my home was all I had left of my parents. Of the life I'd taken for granted and lost in no time at all, and how it was the only real, physical memory I had.

Ben came back then—I felt him return, a sudden burst of tangled thoughts of me, of us. I felt him feel my happiness about my plan, but he didn't return it. His emotions were very strong, but there was something primal about them, something—

Wolf, I thought, and closed my eyes.

Then I opened them and took the picture I'd drawn

down, looking at it closely. There was nothing new in it at all. I was so tired of that. I *had* seen something. It was finding a way to see it again that was my never-ending problem.

Renee picked me up after school but was distracted. The dentist she'd worked for before she'd retired had called because he was having problems in his office.

"His receptionist went to pick up lunch and ended up having to go get her little girl, who has lice." Renee whispered the last word to me. "So she has to take care of her this afternoon, plus run to the drugstore to get the shampoo and things and arrange for—well, anyway, I said I'd go in and answer phones. He's open till seven tonight, to fit in the people who can only come after work. If you don't want me to go, I'll call him—"

"It's okay," I said. "You should go. And I thought of something about the house. About what the council wants to do."

"You did?"

"I'll go and talk to them," I said. "I'll tell them it's all I have left. That if I have to, I'll do whatever they want to make the house so they'll let it stand."

"When Ron came by yesterday," Renee said, touching my knee, "I guess he wasn't clear. The council made its decision. There isn't going to be a meeting. There's not going to be any more discussion. It's going to happen."

"But doesn't what I think matter at all?" I said. "It's

my home! It's all I have left and I haven't even seen it except once. Mom and Dad are gone. Does everything else have to go too? Why can't we go live there? We could fix it, I know it, and they couldn't knock it down then!"

"I'm sorry," Renee said, and her voice cracked. "If I could do anything, I would, I swear. I don't want this either, but we can't move out there. You've been through so much, and to take you back there, to live there? I can't do it. I won't do it."

"But—"

"No," she said. "I can't believe the town would do this, but, well, most of the council members want change. They want Woodlake to grow, and they feel that the only way it can happen is if there's more here. More houses, more shopping, and you know how hard Steve pushes for that. If the town isn't so surrounded by the forest it can grow faster."

"But the land isn't going anywhere," I said, and then looked at Renee. "Is it?"

Her hands tightened on the steering wheel. "I meant what I said before," she said slowly. "I am not selling that land. We are not moving out there, but that land will stay in this family. You can believe me, or you can choose not to. I can't make you trust me."

I remembered everything she'd said to Ron and how upset she'd been when he'd told her about the house, and knew she meant it. She wasn't going to sell Steve all

that would be left of my old life. She wasn't going to sell the land I'd thought I'd be able to visit forever.

She was going to make sure I *could* visit it forever.

"I'm sorry," I said. "I know you wouldn't do that."

"Thank you," she said, her voice soft with surprise. With gratitude.

"I wish you and Dad had talked more, you know. I wish he knew that you understood him."

She was silent for a moment and then said, "Me too," her voice very quiet.

When we got to her house she was reluctant to go so I made a sandwich and ate half of it as she jingled her car keys in her hands, back and forth and back and forth.

I looked at her. "Do you ... besides Dad, are there other things you regret? Things you wish you'd done differently?"

She stilled, and then looked away from me, glanced out into the forest.

"No," she finally said. "I'm too old for regret. But I do need to get going. If you need anything—anything at all—you call me right away and I'll come straight home. If you get lonely or sad or—"

"Thank you," I said, and she kissed the top of my head and then left.

She came back once, right after she'd backed her car down the drive. She said it was because she'd forgotten something, but I knew she wanted to make sure I was okay.

I smiled at her to show I was.

After she left again, I waited five minutes, then ten, and then fifteen.

And then I got up. I had no say in what was going to happen. I'd lost my parents. I was going to lose my home.

So all I had left was the chance to see it now. I was going to go and—

I didn't know. I hadn't been able to fix Mom and Dad. I hadn't been able to save them. I couldn't even save our house, but I could at least see it again.

I could at least remember us—me and Mom and Dad—again.

eighteen

I walked through the woods, cutting into them behind Renee's house, and it wasn't like I didn't know the way. I did.

But all I could think about was how everything was gone. Mom, Dad, and now the house. It was like my whole life was being erased, and I started thinking about what Louis said about power, and how I had it. How the evil that had taken my parents wanted it.

If I had power—whatever it was—the evil must want me. Or it just wanted to make sure I never remembered what happened the night my parents died.

I paused, slowing down. The forest was very quiet. Too quiet? I was pretty sure it was, but then I hadn't been in it every day lately. I wasn't the girl I was before, and in that moment I missed Mom and Dad so much I sank down to the forest floor.

I let the smell of the woods flow into me. I looked at the trees, so constant, forever standing tall, forever standing watch, and wished I had their strength.

I wanted to hear Mom's voice, Dad's voice; I wanted to be walking home and go inside, have Mom remind me to take my shoes off, have Dad ask me if I'd seen anything interesting. I wanted to smell whatever Mom was cooking, and I even wanted to kick off my shoes and watch them land in the pile by the door, the one I was always digging through, trying to find a pair and wondering how it always seemed like one shoe disappeared deep while one was always easy to find.

I wanted Mom to call me over, hug me, and ask me about my day. I wanted her to smile when I said, "Fine," because she knew that meant nothing special had happened; wanted to hear her say, "Tomorrow," like she knew something good would happen then, that something amazing was in store for me.

But all that was gone now.

I got up and started walking again. The forest was still so quiet, but it felt like someone had passed through right before me—or was right behind me.

I stopped and made myself look around. Dad had taught me to track a little, but I couldn't see any signs that someone else had been here. I didn't see any footprints, not even the tiny hints that were left when someone tried to remove them. If anything, the path to the

house seemed like no one ever had been on it. Like I hadn't even been on it.

But I had.

I thought of Ben but pushed it away because I wanted this to be all about my parents. I needed it to be, and I could see the house now, or at least the roof. It shone in the light of the slowly sinking sun, glittered off all the things Dad had used to build it.

I started walking faster, not wanting to see the house like I had before, not in the dark. I want to walk inside in the daylight. I would eat some of Mom's awful trail mix from the pantry at the kitchen table, and then I would . . .

I would do what I knew was right. I would remember them. I might even refuse to leave the house.

I was almost there, and I started walking faster, afraid that I was dreaming, that the town had already made our house disappear.

The sun caught my eyes as I wove around a tree. I let it warm my face for a moment. I hadn't done that since . . . it hurt to even think it. I hadn't let the sun warm my face, something so simple, so easy, since before my parents died.

I had thought of the forest, wanted to be in it, and even had been in it, but I hadn't stopped to truly *be* in it. Not like I used to. Not like Mom and Dad had taught me to.

I closed my eyes and heard the wind blow. I listened

to the woods, and remembered what it was like to have everything come to me through the forest. I heard the trees shift as the wind changed and listened to them creak, their branches groaning, a deep, hollow sound I had only heard the time Dad and I had been out walking and saw an old tree drop one of its branches.

This was different, though. It was louder and sounded strange, forced somehow.

I opened my eyes, and saw a tree falling.

It was falling right toward me, and it was a healthy tree, not a dead one, which are the ones that usually fall. And not only was it healthy, it was huge, with branches that could snare and flay me open, and a trunk that could break me in two.

I saw it coming and it was moving fast—so fast, hurtling toward me. I could actually see the leaves on the tree now and they were still green, they were still alive. But if they were, then why—?

And then something hit me, hard, and I flew—actually flew—through the air, heard the loud *whoosh* of the tree hitting the ground, saw the earth shake. Sensed it as I landed.

I looked up, terrified, confused—and saw Ben looking back at me, his chest heaving as he breathed, his eyes wild.

"I—the tree," I said, but didn't look at it. I couldn't. I could only see Ben.

"Someone cut it," he said, his voice harsh. "Someone came through here and did this, killed this tree and left it so it would fall on whoever walked by. This was— someone planned this very carefully. Avery, someone tried to kill you."

nineteen

Kill me?" I said. "Ben, why would . . . ?" I trailed off at the look on his face, at how his fists were bunched by his sides, tension practically vibrating off him. He was angry, but under that, around it, he was scared for me.

And I felt that.

"For the land," I whispered.

"Yes," he said. And then he held a hand out toward me, an offer to help me up.

I knew what had happened the other night. I knew what I'd felt from Ben. I knew what he'd felt from me. I knew what taking his hand would mean to him.

I knew what it meant to me.

I took his hand.

He was so strong that when I rose, we ended up standing right next to each other. Close enough to touch.

Close enough to kiss.

He looked at me, and he was still shaking with worry, with rage, and I needed to calm him down, wanted him to know I was safe. What I felt for him was already so strong, so fierce. I yearned for him to hold me and I could tell he felt that, watched as his eyes widened. He stared at my mouth then and swayed toward me, his own mouth opening a little.

I needed him to touch me, to kiss me, and he needed it too.

I knew that because I could sense his want, I could sense *him*. I stilled and looked at him, suddenly wondering something.

"How old are you?"

"Seventeen," he said.

"Seventeen for how long?" My voice shook.

"Six months. Why?"

"You're two months younger than me? But you— you should be older, right? Like hundreds of years older."

"I'm not . . . I age like you do," Ben said. "I'm seventeen now, and then I'll turn eighteen. Then nineteen. Avery, I'm not going to live forever or anything like that. And what you felt that night on my back only comes when I've—when I'm about to change or just have."

He took another step toward me, so close that there was only the tiniest bit of space between us, and then stopped, like he didn't trust himself.

And then he took his shirt off.

I sucked in a breath, staring, my whole body melting as he turned, his face turning faintly red, a blush coloring his high cheekbones. His body was—

It was beautiful. And his back looked normal. Human.

I wanted to touch it, and he must have sensed that because he exhaled fast, his face flushed and his breathing hard as he put his shirt back on. "Let me walk you back to your grandmother's."

"Because I'm not safe here?"

He looked at the tree that had landed on the ground, saying everything without words.

I looked right back at him, unable to believe someone would do that. How would they have even known I was coming out here? "Trees fall. Even healthy ones."

"Not like this," he said, and moved toward the tree. I followed, and he reached out a hand to help me. I looked at it, then him.

I had kissed him before, I'd wanted him, but this was about more than that.

This was about trust.

I took his hand again. His skin was warm, his palms rough, like he'd spent time working with wood.

Or running through the woods like a wolf did.

He led me over to the tree's base, but he didn't have to show me what was there. I could see it. Someone

had hacked at it, broken it. Killed it, and then left it to fall.

I ran a hand over the crude, harsh cuts in the wood, seeing the delicate rings that had been exposed and the space left for more, the slow growing. The tree had years of life left. Centuries, even. And now it was gone.

"How did it fall like it did?" I whispered.

"It was cut so deep it was ready to," Ben said. "It just needed the pressure of someone passing by to fall. Who knew you were coming out here?"

"No one."

"Are you sure?"

"Yeah, I'm sure. I know I didn't tell anyone."

Ben closed his eyes. "But this ... whoever did this is someone who knows you. Who else would know that you'd come out here but someone who knew you'd have a reason to?"

"The town council voted to tear the house down, and I wanted to see it before it happened. So I guess they all could have figured that out." I looked at the house, so close, and took a step toward it, but Ben touched my arm.

"You can't go in there," he said. "If someone killed this tree to try and kill you, then there's bound to be something waiting inside your parents' house. It's too dangerous to go in there."

"It's not."

"It is," he said, softening his voice. "Who exactly in town wants the house gone? If we know that, then maybe we'll know who killed your parents."

I froze then, and stared at him. "We?"

"Avery," he said, and as he said my name I heard music in it. I heard want in it, and it made me shiver. Not from cold. Not from fear.

But from the idea of us together.

I swayed toward him and he inhaled, sharply, and put his hands on my arms. Lightly, so lightly, but I could feel them. Feel *him*.

"Don't," he said, his voice a tortured whisper. "We have to—who knew about the house?"

"Everyone, like I said," I told him, surprised that he didn't know how Woodlake was, but then I remembered it was still new to him. He hadn't been here that long, but I truly believed part of me had known him forever. Like I'd been waiting for him my whole life.

"Everyone knows?"

"It's a small town. There aren't secrets," I said. "Not many anyway, and I came out here to do this. So I am doing it."

I moved away from him and took another step toward the house.

"You'll die if you do," Ben said, grabbing my arm. "I can feel that there are bad things in that house."

"Like what?"

"Things that will hurt you. That want to hurt you. There's . . . something there."

"But you don't *know* that," I said. "You feel it, right? And you can be wrong about what you feel, can't you? I mean, there definitely was something awful there, but why would it still be there?"

"You're right," he whispered, and once again he'd managed to surprise me by saying something I hadn't expected him to say at all. I stared at him, stunned, and he closed his eyes briefly before opening them and looking at me again.

"It's just that I thought—I thought my family was safe," he said. "We lived in a town a lot like this one, only farther north, up near the Canadian border. My father was part of a pack when he was young, but after he met my mom and I was born, he wanted us to live on our own. He said it was safer, and so we lived out in the woods, just the five of us. There was a town nearby—Little Falls— and we went sometimes but no one ever—no one ever knew about us. About who we were. My father was so happy about that and I never wondered why."

He blew out a breath. "I wish I had. I went out one night, out to . . . to change, and I thought about them. I thought about my mother, my father, my little sisters, and when I did, I sensed that things were fine. But when I came back the next morning, they were dead. Murdered."

"Murdered?"

"Yes," he said, his voice bitter. "There are some people, Hunters, who think all things they can't understand, that aren't human, are evil. So they tracked us and ... and they found us. We were all alone, just the five of us, but that didn't matter, not to the Hunters. Somehow they found my family, and they killed them all, even my little sisters. They killed them all even though we'd never hurt anyone, Avery. Not ever."

"And so you came here to live with Louis," I whispered, and he nodded.

"He was the only family Dad kept in touch with. The Hunters are—Dad worried about them. Too much, I thought, but I was wrong. I was so wrong."

"I'm sorry," I said, and touched his shoulder. I knew how he felt, how huge his loss was. I could feel his grief for his parents, for his family, and his regret that he hadn't sensed something was happening. His rage over what had happened. So many emotions, and there was something elemental about them, something not human, but I still recognized them.

I still felt for him, but I had to try and understand what had happened. I had to—I had to think clearly. Or as clearly as I could.

"How did you know about today?" I said, drawing my hand away. "How did you know about the tree?"

"I didn't. Not until I saw it start to fall. That's

why I think you should stay away from the house. Something—someone—is after you. I do know that for sure."

"Did ... did you follow me?"

"No," he said. "I was in the forest already. I was running."

I looked at him. His clothes had no sweat stains on them. His moccasins looked a little scuffed, but I knew that was from how he'd moved when he'd pushed me out of the way. My father had gone running in the woods and he'd always returned sweat-stained and covered with bits of leaves, decorated with smudges of the forest. Ben's clothes looked as if they hadn't been run in at all. As if they'd been left behind.

Dropped when he changed.

"Running?" I said, and he looked at me.

He looked at me, and I knew for certain that he hadn't run as Ben, but as the other part of himself. The part that wasn't human.

"But your back," I said. "It's not—the little patch isn't there."

"I changed a while ago," he said. "I had changed back and was heading to Louis's. I'd promised him that I'd spend the day trying not to think about you, because how you can feel my emotions and I can feel yours—it isn't supposed to happen."

"So you can stop it?" I said, and heard my voice crack,

tears stinging my eyes. It was stupid to be surprised by this, to be hurt by it, but I was.

"I don't know," he said. "Louis asked me to try. But I don't . . . I don't want to stop. That's what I realized today. I felt your emotions the first time I saw you, and I've never felt anything like it before. Not from someone else, and not even from someone like me."

"You mean you've known girls who are . . ." I couldn't say it. I didn't want to think it. And not because I didn't believe it, but because I did.

I was jealous. The idea of Ben and someone like him? I didn't like that. The idea of Ben and anyone else . . . I didn't like that at all either.

He nodded. "I have. A pack was living in Little Falls when my family . . . when they died. But with you . . . Avery, the minute I saw you, I wanted to be near you. To be with you."

I could sense—no, I was part of—everything he felt behind those words: relief that I was safe, that the tree hadn't hurt me. Happiness, because I was talking to him and because I hadn't turned away from him like Louis had said I would.

I felt all that he did, and it was amazing. I didn't care what he was. He was Ben, and I cared about him. I needed him.

"Oh," he said, a shocked, pained sound, and then I was suddenly aware of something dark, something evil,

nearby, a swift cold shiver running not just down my spine but all through me.

And it—whatever it was—was thinking about me. Wanted to find me.

I closed my eyes, willing it to go away. But it wouldn't. It was willing to wait.

It was willing to wait for me as long as it had to.

twenty

"Y ou felt that too?" Ben said, and pulled me into his arms.

"Yes," I said softly. Numbly.

"Whatever it is, it's angry. It wants the land, and Louis says your parents might have—" He kissed the top of my head, reluctant to ask what I knew he was going to. "Did either of your parents say anything that could have upset someone?"

"Enough to kill?"

"Yes."

"No, not my parents. They were nice. Like, really nice. It's not possible," I said, and then I thought about Dad.

Dad, with his opinions on everything. Dad, who said whatever he wanted and didn't care what people thought; who spoke out against every proposed expansion of Woodlake; who'd argued that what made Woodlake special was

the fact it wasn't easy to get to, that it wasn't like everywhere else.

"Something happened," Ben whispered. "What was it?"

"Don't," I said, and pushed him away. "I don't want—
you might sense what I feel, but they're my feelings.
Mine."

"I didn't mean to. I can't help it. This is what a connection—a bond—is. You feel things strongly and I feel
them too."

I took a deep breath, wanting him to understand what
I was saying. "You know all this stuff about being con-
nected, about having a bond and stuff, but it's all new to
me. Everything's changed so fast."

"I know," Ben said. "And if things were different, there
would be more time for both of us to get used to this. But
I can't slow it down. You're in my head, you're in my heart,
and I've lost so much already. I can't lose you too."

His worry washed over me, and his sorrow that I was
upset. His fear that I would reject him.

"Louis said I could stop this—stop us," I said. "I'd just
have to not think about you at all. Is that true?"

Ben flinched.

"Yes," he said after a moment, his voice tight. "He was
right. It'll go away if you stop thinking about me. You
tried it earlier today."

"You felt that?"

"I couldn't—you were gone," he said, and behind us,

the fallen tree creaked one last groan as the wind blew through it. "Louis told me to try and get ready for that. He said to try and stop thinking about you because you'd do it. He's seen it happen before."

I thought of Louis, who'd lived alone for as long as I'd known him, but who'd spoken, with something deep and sad in his voice, of a long-ago girl supposedly like me.

"It happened to him, didn't it?" I said.

Ben nodded. "He likes you, but you aren't the safest choice for me."

"And you are for me?"

"No, I'm not," he said slowly. "So if you want to end it, you should."

"What happens to me if I do?" Louis had said I'd be fine, but Louis wasn't Ben. Ben was who I trusted.

"Nothing."

"Ben," I whispered. "I can feel there's something else. Something you aren't saying. What is it?"

He was silent, and I looked at him.

"I trust you," I said. "Do you trust me?"

He swallowed, then said, "Yes. If you stop, you'll be fine, but I won't be able to. I can try, but I'll always be pulled toward you. Toward the things you feel most deeply. Once a bond happens, it can't be undone, just . . . broken if the other person is human. Louis says the pain fades over time, that not feeling the other person's emotions gets easier to live with."

"So you'd think about me forever?"

"Yes," Ben said and I sensed his sadness even as I felt his willingness to let me go no matter what. Even if it broke him.

I didn't want it to end. My parents loved me, of course, but no one had ever understood me like Ben did.

No one would, because no one else would ever be able to feel what I was thinking like he could.

No one else would ever let me see into their heart like he could.

Like he did.

I didn't want that to end.

He felt that, felt my choice, and his joy slammed into me, making my legs shake, and then he was holding me.

He moved so fast; he moved like no one else ever could, and then his mouth touched mine and an entire world bloomed there.

A world where it was just us, and the forest approved—I was aware of the trees shifting even though the wind wasn't blowing; I knew they could sense us and tossed leaves down toward us, a shower to cradle us.

Ben kissed me like he could kiss me forever, like he had to kiss me forever and he wanted to, he wanted me, and when he felt my surprise at that, I could feel again how beautiful I was to him, how I was beautiful beyond words.

He blushed when he sensed how I saw him, his face

turning red, his whole body going warm under my hands as I clung to him, and he didn't believe it, he couldn't believe I felt like that, but I did and I knew it and now he did too.

He shivered, and I felt the muscles of his back twitch, felt them become longer, leaner.

He gasped, pushed away from me.

"Ben?" I said, and he shook his head, said, "I want to be with you so much I don't know if I ... I don't know what might happen."

"Ben," I said again, wanting him back in my arms. I reached for him, knowing him, knowing he sensed what emotions were driving me. That all of me was alive in a way I'd never been before. That I wanted him.

Off in the distance, a wolf howled, a short, sharp bark, and I froze.

He didn't know what would happen if things between us went further.

He meant he didn't know if he'd stay human.

"I'd never hurt you," he said, and I could almost touch his hope.

His fear.

We looked at each other. I felt a million things, and he felt them all too, and it was—

It was too much, and hadn't Louis said something about me and power?

Why couldn't I try to use that power, whatever it was?

Why didn't I go and try to use it—why didn't I do what I'd come here for?

"No," Ben said as I started walking, and then said it again, louder.

I turned back and looked at him.

"I have to go," I said. "This—my parents and my home—is why I came out here. I can't forget that. I won't."

twenty-one

Ben grabbed my arm, and when he did I sensed that inside the house—

I felt something inside the house, I felt it through Ben, and it was *hate*. Pure and simple and so, so strong.

Hate directed at the woods. At me.

The thing that wanted me dead had been there—and recently—just as surely as it had set up the tree that had almost hit me, planning everything so I'd be dead.

I'd be dead now if it wasn't for Ben.

I pulled away from him then, shaking, and stared out into the woods.

"It's not there anymore, but I can feel it. It was there, it was in the house. It did—" I pointed at the fallen tree. "Will it ever stop?"

"I don't know," Ben said.

"And you—what about us? What do we do now?"

I knew his answer before he said it, sensed his confusion right before he whispered, "I don't know," again.

"Why did it end for Louis and the girl he loved?" I said and saw Ben shift. I knew he had been told something he didn't want to tell me.

"What happened?"

"She saw him," he finally said. "She came to see him, and he wasn't—"

"He wasn't human," I said.

Ben closed his eyes and then nodded.

"Show me," I said. "Show me now."

His eyes flew open. "I can't."

"Why?"

Off in the distance, the wolf cried again, this time longer, deeper. Sharper.

"Avery, that part of me isn't something I . . . I'm not calm around you. I'm not in control, and if I change—"

"You might hurt me?"

He swallowed. "I would do everything, anything, not to."

It was an answer and yet no answer at all. I felt his worry, his fear, and under it was something else, something I'd sensed before. Something different.

Something not human.

Something that wanted to take over Ben, and wanted to do it right now.

"You should go," Ben said, shuddering. His eyes

flashed silver, so bright and so inhuman, right as his whole body seemed to ripple, shift.

"Go," he said again, pleading this time, and I did.

I did because everything I'd wanted to see today had—it hadn't happened. Everything had changed. Shattered.

I ran back through the woods, back to Renee's house, half afraid that Ben would come after me, half afraid he wouldn't.

He didn't, and I walked into my grandmother's house, then sank down onto the floor and cried again.

I cried because I had thought I was so close to Ben, but had ended up running away yet again, afraid of what lay inside him. Afraid of what he—

What he was.

I cried because I trusted him, because I knew he cared, and I had thought that was enough. Wasn't trust and caring supposed to be everything? Maybe, but for us it was more complicated than that.

I cried because I'd needed to go home and I hadn't, and now I knew—

Now I knew that I never would again.

twenty-two

I made sure I was up in the guest room when Renee came back, sat at the desk she'd set up for me and stared at a book, pretending I was reading it.

"You want to watch a little TV with me?" Renee said.

I shook my head. I'd cried so much that my voice had faded, my sobs becoming ragged, hoarse. And then silent. I was so tired of being sad and confused about everything, especially Ben.

But I had no idea what to do. I just . . . I *felt*.

"Oh. Well, all right," Renee said and then paused. "Is everything okay?"

"Just tired."

Renee touched my shoulder. "You come find me if you need anything or if you want to talk or just watch TV, all right?"

I nodded and she left. I remembered the house, and

how much I'd hoped to find some peace or at least sense Mom and Dad and me as we were, to really go home and feel that I was home.

But it hadn't happened. It was as if all of it had happened to someone else because now all the things I'd loved had been tainted. I was so aware of what had been in the house, of what wanted me, and I hated the thought of it touching my parents' things. Of it seeing and being surrounded by what was left of my old life.

It had taken what had been and twisted it, turned it all inside out, upside down.

I put the book I'd been fake reading down. *Romeo and Juliet.* It had come over from the house, *my* house, a play I'd read with Mom back in eighth grade, struggling to understand why it was so great until we'd watched a movie based on it. I got it as soon as I watched the movie, as soon as the action on-screen made the words that were so foreign come to life. I realized the play was about a love that went beyond everything—

Why had I even picked this up? I had actual reading to do, actual homework. I still needed to read Milton, finish his long poem about paradise and Satan and temptation and—

And falling from grace. Losing everything.

I didn't want to read anything now. I didn't even want to think about reading.

I got into bed even though it was early. I didn't think

I'd sleep but I did. I dreamed of the forest. I dreamed of my parents, saw them sitting at the kitchen table smiling at each other and then at me. I saw my mother waving before I went outside into the dark.

And then I was outside, in that sudden way dreams shift, and the woods were all around me, but they were different. It was as if they knew something, as if they were sure something was coming.

I tried to go back to the house but I couldn't move. I was trapped, and then . . .

And then Ben came up to me. Whispered, "Avery," and wrapped his hands around my waist, pulling me close.

"I need you," he said. "And you can't stay away from me, can you?"

I looked at him and knew I couldn't. I leaned in, wanting him to kiss me, and right as his lips were about to touch mine I couldn't see him anymore. All I could see was red.

But it wasn't red, it was blood, rivers of it everywhere, blood all over me, and my mother was there, just out of reach and staring at me, fear and surprise in her eyes.

I said, "Mommy?" but she didn't blink, she didn't see me, she didn't look at me at all, she was seeing something else, and I saw . . .

I saw silver, gleaming, moving so fast, so—inhumanly—over and over.

I woke up then, slapped a hand over my mouth to

stifle a scream, and sat there, shivering in the dark. I wanted to remember everything that happened but yet—

I was glad that I didn't. I was ashamed of myself, mad at myself for it, but it didn't change a thing. I was glad because the horror I'd felt in the dream was . . .

I knew it had been even worse for real. I knew what I'd seen was beyond horrible.

My mind was closed for a reason, and part of me wanted it to stay that way.

twenty-three

I got up before my alarm went off, got dressed, grabbed my bag, and then went downstairs. I needed school today, needed to get away from my thoughts.

I needed, more than anything, to get away from myself, and the routine of classes and all that went with them would help. It would let me pretend there was one normal thing in my life.

Renee was up when I came downstairs, of course, and she gave me a look as I came into the kitchen, where she was sitting at the table with a mug of coffee and looking out the sliding glass door. It was partly open, fresh forest air flowing in.

I smiled at her and got out a bowl for cereal I didn't really want to eat.

"What are you doing?" she said, getting up and closing the sliding glass door.

"Breakfast. Do you not want me to eat cereal?"

"No," she said, and looked away from the woods, looked at me, her face troubled. "It's Saturday. You don't have school today."

Saturday. No school. Just a whole day here with Renee and the memories of yesterday, of the forest. Of my house.

Of the tree.

Of Ben.

Of the dream I'd had about Ben. And the blood.

"Right," I said, and made myself smile. "I guess I just forgot."

"You can go back to bed," Renee said, but I sat down, shoving my book bag under my chair so it was out of sight. So maybe Renee wouldn't worry.

It was too late for that, though. I could tell she already was.

"I'm not really sleepy," I said, trying to be normal, hoping I could pull it off, and her gaze sharpened, taking in what I knew was my drained-looking face. My haunted eyes.

"You know, we should do something today," I said, so she wouldn't say anything about what I'd just done, how I'd forgotten what day it was. So she wouldn't ask any questions I didn't want to answer. "Something fun."

"Well, that sounds good, but you seem a little—"

"I need to do something," I said. "I need to not think about things today. Okay?" I heard the pleading note in my voice, and Renee did too.

Her face softened and she sat down too, reached across the table and patted my hand.

"Then we will," she said. "What do you like to do for fun?"

"I..." I said, and then stopped. I didn't know anymore. I'd spent every moment with my parents until last year and then I'd gone to school. That had taught me a lot about how people were, but not very much about fun, or at least the kind of things I'd thought were fun, and then— well, then everything else had happened.

Ben, I thought and pictured us sitting together. Just that, talking and sitting, and that...

That would be fun.

I shoved the thought away.

"I like to walk in the woods," I said.

"I do too, but I think we need to do something else besides that," Renee said. "Something that isn't about that forest. Something that won't make us think about your parents."

So we ended up working on the porch. It turned out neither one of us wanted to go shopping—I hated the mall the one time I'd been to it with Kirsta, and after Renee brought it up as something we could do and I'd shaken my head, she said, "Oh, thank goodness. I hate driving out there, I hate the parking lot, and I hate all the weird lighting."

"Me too," I said. "I hate how fake it all is."

"Do you wish you liked it?" Renee said.

"No. My parents taught me to be who I am and I'm glad they did."

"Me too," Renee said. "I think I'll put you in charge of putting together the swing."

"The swing?"

"A porch swing," she said, smiling. "So we can sit and look at the stars and the forest. Not much point to a porch if you can't sit on it, right?"

I'd never had to sit somewhere to look at the forest. I'd always been able to go into it.

I started to say that, and then I remembered last night and closed my eyes.

Just one day was all I wanted. Just one normal, ordinary day. *I can have that*, I told myself. *I really can.*

"All right," I said, opening my eyes. "Show me the swing."

Renee did, and it was a lot harder to put together than I'd thought. There were tons of pieces, most of which looked alike, and they all had to be screwed together with a tiny metal thing that kept sliding out of my hands.

"Dad would have hated this thing," I said, as I struggled to put post J into slot K.

"What?" Renee said, distracted-sounding. She'd just come back from the house, where she'd gone to answer the phone. I wondered who'd called, but didn't ask.

I just said, "Are you all right?"

She shook her head and said, "Ron just called to

check in. He said he'd heard there was someone out by your parents' house yesterday, and that a tree fell near it. It could have killed someone, actually, and he just wanted to make sure you weren't out there when it happened."

She paused for a moment and then looked at me. "I said you weren't."

I stared at the swing, plucking my fingers over the very stubborn piece labeled J.

"I don't want to lose anyone else I love," she said. "I couldn't bear it. Do you understand?"

"I do," I said, and looked right at her. "And if I can ever remember who killed my parents, I can at least know that whoever did it won't hurt anyone else. I have to stay alive for that to happen."

"Plus you have college too," she said. "You'll have to think about that pretty soon. And about the rest of your life. Right?"

"I—yes," I said to her, but I hadn't thought of college for ages, too caught up in what had happened to my parents.

Too caught up in Ben.

Renee looked at me for a moment, and then she said, "You do need to think about that, you know. About your future."

"About leaving here?" I said, thinking of all the fights she and Dad had over this, over how she wanted him to do more, be more. How it had broken them.

"No," she said, her voice soft. "Just . . . you can't live in the past. Trust me, it only brings pain." She looked away, then said, "All right, let's get back to it. Okay?"

I looked at her. I remembered the pain I knew she'd had—losing Dad not once, but twice. I wondered about the pain I didn't know about but could tell was there.

Renee and I were still getting to know each other, and I realized we were still working on building a relationship, on building trust.

"Okay," I said, and went back to work.

It took me most of the day, but I ended up getting the porch swing together. Renee and I had worked hard, only stopping to throw together a sandwich around noon, and as I used the weird little wrench/whatever it was to put the last screw in, my stomach rumbled.

"Let's go out to dinner," Renee said. "I'm so tired from dealing with all this wood, plus we both deserve a treat. How do you feel about Bessie's?"

"Okay," I said, and grinned, thinking of the restaurant. It was the only one in Woodlake, but me and Mom and Dad almost never went there. Maybe once a year, on my birthday, and Dad would always say nothing tasted as good as what Mom made, but I loved it. I loved seeing the people in it. Before I went to school, the only time I was ever around stuff like that—around what people who lived what Dad called "boring" lives did—was when I went into town and to places like Bessie's.

"I should go change, right?" I said and Renee laughed and said, "Why? It's just Bessie's."

She'd been there a lot. She'd had a town life, a normal life. One Dad wouldn't have wanted. I hesitated, wondering what he and Mom would think about this.

"I used to see your mother at Bessie's, you know," Renee said.

"Mom?"

"Oh, not on purpose or anything," Renee said. "But I'd go in for lunch sometimes and she'd be there. She liked their brownie sundae. We used to talk."

"You and Mom?" I stared at Renee. "But she never said—"

"Your father wouldn't have been happy," she said. "But Debby and I both loved John and we both loved you. And I like a good brownie sundae myself."

"You and Mom talked?"

"Just a few times," Renee said. "Your parents followed their own path, you know, and you can follow yours. You should. That's what they'd want. They loved you like parents should." She looked down at the ground and I knew she was thinking about Dad. They'd fought so hard and for so long that only silence was left between them, a silence that had never been broken.

"All right," I said, and we headed toward the car. I looked at the porch swing, swaying gently in the breeze that blew across Renee's yard as we backed down the

driveway. I could see the reflection of her car in the glass of her kitchen door, and even saw the newspaper Renee had been reading in the morning on the table.

The *paper.*

Is that why—could that be why my parents had died? Ben had asked if my parents had ever upset anyone, and Dad had definitely done that, had made some people in Woodlake angry with his articles and editorials always arguing for what no one else would.

But enough to kill over?

That wasn't possible. It just wasn't.

And then I remembered his last big crusade, the one that the town council had been talking about too. The one that, for once, Dad and the council had agreed on.

Wolves.

Dad had been writing newspaper articles arguing in favor of allowing wolf hunting.

"Oh," I whispered as the thought really hit me, washed over me, and Renee said, "What is it?"

"Nothing. I was just thinking. Dad's last articles were about wolf hunting."

"They were? Oh, right," Renee said. "He actually agreed with the town council for the first time ever. Everyone was talking about that more than anything else, actually."

She said something else but I didn't hear her. All I could see was Ben pushing away from me, saying he

wouldn't hurt me, but that didn't change the fact that part of him wasn't—

Part of him didn't think like a human.

Part of him *wasn't* human.

And what if someone like him came to town and found out he might be hunted along with our wolves too? That he could be killed like his family had been killed?

Louis would have known about the council's plans. He would have told Ben, if for no other reason than to make sure he stayed safe. And while Louis hardly left his house, Ben . . .

Ben did.

And Ben knew where my parents lived. I'd found him in the house.

I went into Bessie's with Renee, but I wasn't hungry anymore. I picked at the salad that came before our food, telling myself to calm down.

And then I saw Ben.

twenty-four

I tensed, my fork clattering along the side of my salad plate, and wished I could pretend I hadn't seen him.

I wanted to get up and go to him. I wanted . . .

I wanted to know what to do, but I didn't. Everything was still strange, upside down, backward—confusing.

"Here you go," the waitress said, putting our food in front of us, and I stared at the sandwich I must have ordered, at the pieces of roast beef that had been piled high, the edges of it spilling out of the bread.

"That looks good," Renee said, taking a bite of her chicken sandwich, and I looked at the roast beef again. I saw the way the meat—not overcooked, but still a soft red in the center—lay there.

I saw the little puddle of juice that was coming off it and sliding over the plate.

But it wasn't juice, and I knew that.

It was blood.

Blood, red blood, and I said, "I have to go to the bath-room," and got up, needing to get away from the table and my food.

I needed to get away from Ben, who was still there, and who I wanted to see but didn't know if I should.

I didn't go in the ladies' room. I walked by it and down the narrow hallway. One door, swinging open and closed, led into the kitchen. The other was closed.

Closed, but not locked.

I opened it and stepped out into the narrow alley between Bessie's and the dress store—Sharon's—that was next door. There were trash bins down at the end of the alley, mostly filled with empty boxes. Everyone said Bessie's food was too good to not eat all of it, and that was how I'd always felt when I'd gone there, always eat-ing every last bite.

I couldn't eat anything now.

I leaned against the wall, rough brick at my back, and looked up at the stars, making myself take deep breaths like Mom had taught me to do whenever I got upset. I'd always thought it was stupid—I knew how to breathe— but she was right. Sometimes you did have to slow down and think about it. Sometimes you—

Sometimes you could get so turned around that even breathing became complicated.

The stars were harder to see in town. I couldn't make

out any of the Milky Way at all and it was strange to not be able to see it, to not really see the stars and how they fit into the enormous pattern of light and energy that surrounded us.

I had to go back inside. I knew that. I'd ask to take my sandwich home, say I was too tired to eat and then throw it away as soon as I could. I wouldn't think about blood or what it reminded me of. How it made me think of everything I couldn't remember.

How I'd been found covered in it, and how it was my last memory of the life I'd had.

"Avery."

Ben. I stilled, and looked at him. He'd somehow come down the alley so quietly I hadn't heard him, but of course he could do that.

He was standing near me, so close that I could look into his eyes. So close I could reach out and touch him.

"I didn't hear you," I said, and then thought not of him, but of how the forests' wolves ran at night and how I had once spotted two of them out my window at home. They were so quiet that even with the crack in my wall I'd heard nothing but the night.

I'd heard nothing at all.

"You were thinking," Ben said, smiling. He was holding a bag from Bessie's, the name printed in bright yellow on the plastic. It seemed so strange to see him here. To see him with food when he could just go out and—

He could just go out and find his own. Hunt it down.

I remembered my sandwich again, remembered the blood dripping from it, and my stomach twisted.

"What's wrong?" Ben said, his voice soft, urgent. "Something's scared you, made you unhappy."

"And can you *feel* why?" I said and Ben swallowed, looked at the ground.

"I know it's about your parents."

"Yes, but that's not all," I said, and he flinched like I'd hit him.

"Avery, I meant what I said. I'd do anything to avoid hurting you."

"Part of you might," I said, and pointed at the moon, which hung low in the sky, full and heavy. A low, red moon. "You were here when my parents died. Did you know my father was going to support hunting to reduce the wolf population?"

"No," Ben said. "And even if I did know, those kinds of hunters aren't the kind that killed my family." His mouth tightened. "You said you trusted me before. What changed that?"

"You can change into something that isn't human," I said. "You're . . . you're a wolf."

"No," he said. "I'm not. It's part of who I am, but it's not all I am. And you didn't answer my question."

Now it was my turn to look at the ground. "I started thinking about my father's articles. About the things he'd said about wolf hunting."

I looked up at the sky. "Shouldn't you be—isn't tonight—won't you . . . change?"

He laughed, and it stung.

I sensed his sorrow for that even as I could feel his amusement swimming through my mind, as I felt an undercurrent of something else behind it.

Sadness.

"Those are stories, Avery," he said. "I'm real and the moon has nothing to do with when I change. Maybe you and I are crazy, maybe we aren't supposed to be together, but that doesn't mean we can't be. And if you don't trust me anymore, why are you still out here with me?"

"Because I . . . because I want to be. Because I do—" I blew out a breath, then whispered, "I do believe in you. In us. And I do trust you."

He didn't ask me if I meant it. He didn't need to. I knew he could feel that I did. He smiled and I saw it, watched it change his face.

I saw it make him look even more beautiful.

"Thank you," he said. "I . . . you and me, all of this, it's all new to me too, you know."

"I know," I said, because I did. "So all the stories I've heard about you and the moon and things like that—none of them are true?"

"Well, if I change when the moon is full, I can't change back until sunrise even if I try," he said slowly. "That's the one hold the moon does have over us. Me."

"Can I ask you something else?" I said. "Wait, don't answer that. I'm going to ask anyway. Why do you do this?" I pointed at his Bessie's bag. "Doesn't part of you hate this? Hate eating food instead of catching it?"

"No," he said, and his shock at my question rolled over me. "Eating food from Bessie's is part of who I am. What I can do, what happens to me, it's part of me too, but I'm—Avery, you know how I feel. You know exactly how human I am. You know it better than anyone else ever has. You—" He smiled. "I trust you too. So I'll tell you whatever you want."

"How do you—what is it like to chan—?" I started to say, and then everything that lay between us hit me. Ben was human, but he wasn't totally human. He was part wolf, a legend that was real, and even if everything about full moons wasn't true, some stories were.

Stories I hadn't known about. Stories I still didn't know much about. My mind was spinning and—

Silver, gleaming.

"What is it?" Ben said. "I can tell you're thinking about something else."

"Silver," I said, my voice soft.

"Silver bullets, right? That's a myth too. I really am just like you. Anything that can hurt you can hurt me." He touched his chest. "My heart beats just like yours."

I knew I should have told him what I'd seen then.

I wanted to tell him about the silver. He'd sensed the evil around my parents' house. We both had. And he might know what the silver meant.

And then I looked at him and saw silver gleaming in his brown eyes. I watched them shift, flare bright, and then go back to brown again.

When that happened, the shining web of trust between us began to shift a little.

Crack a little.

"My eyes," he said. "You saw that? I . . ." He trailed off in surprise. Shock.

Fear.

I nodded.

"Humans aren't supposed to be able to see that."

"Well, I did."

"You're special," he said, his voice full of awe, his eyes wide. "The connection we have is—I get that, but you can see the wolf in people. Do you know how rare that is? I was always told it was a myth. You're not . . . you're not supposed to be real."

I had to smile at that. Me, mythical.

Me, talking to someone who actually was. "Neither are you."

He smiled back, and it changed the tense look on his face, made him look like something from out of a story.

But Ben was real, he was here, and he took a step toward me.

I didn't move away. I didn't move because I did trust him.

"Have you seen anyone else like me?" he said. "Out in the forest or anywhere else?"

"Just Louis, but I knew because he's your great-uncle and not from his eyes, although I did see silver in them. Was I supposed to see that?"

Ben shook his head.

"Oh," I said. "Have you seen other people like you here?"

He shook his head again. "No, but the woods are so big Louis says there must be others. Not family, but still. I haven't seen any. And I haven't really been looking." He looked at me. "Not lately, anyway."

"Do you want to?"

"I did," he whispered. "When I first came here. I hoped I'd find someone who would understand. Someone who'd see me."

He touched my cheek, one finger sliding down it. "And then I saw you."

"But I'm not—"

"No," he said. "You're not like me. But Avery, I want—" He broke off and leaned in toward me, mouth descending toward mine.

I froze, waiting. Hoping.

I did trust him, and this—with him—was where I wanted to be.

I felt his breath brush across my lips and then turn, moving over my cheek to my ear and then down to my neck.

His mouth hovered there. I waited, felt him almost touching his lips to my skin, felt him breathing against me, and I should have been scared.

Ben wasn't human, and I knew what wolves did when they caught their prey. I knew how open and vulnerable my neck was, how he could—

But he wouldn't. My heart knew what he'd said was true. He'd never hurt me.

Ben ran his mouth almost—but not quite—over my neck, like he was breathing me in, like I was something he had to be close to.

"Avery," he said, his voice cracking. He was thinking about before now, about when we'd kissed, when we'd touched, and he wanted it all again. He craved me, and he was trying to be strong, he was, but the way he saw me—

He made me seem so beautiful. Everything about me, from my hair to my skin to the way I smelled, like the woods and forever—and his mind caught on that, on me, and he would never forget that I smelled like forever to him, like wanting and hope and everything that was possible all rolled together.

"You're sniffing me," I said, and he was. That part of him, that primal part—it liked what it smelled, it liked

me. It wanted me too, and I sensed its wanting pushing through Ben's feelings, pure and raw, and I gasped, lifted my hands up and touched his shoulders.

Every part of Ben needed me, called to me. I couldn't think and didn't want to because I wanted him too. I'd been drawn to him since the first time I'd seen him. So why not give in? Why not let this all happen?

"Yes," he said, and his voice was lower, not like a growl but just deeper, full of power, but he shook his head, hard, his eyes flaring bright, bright silver as he took a step back, as far away from me as he could.

It wasn't very far. The alley was narrow.

"If I touch you now, I'm afraid I could change," he said, and that primal wanting was still there and he was worried because what would happen if he changed?

What would happen if I saw him as he could be, as he sometimes was, as he sometimes had to be?

I'd seen wolves. I'd seen them all my life.

I remembered that photo Dad had brought home for me to see, of the wolf that had been wandering through town, Dad telling me it proved the stories weren't real and how I'd been so sure that wolf was lonely.

Lonely, scared—just like Ben was now. I felt his fear, his want, how alone he'd been since his parents died, how alone he'd always been because there was supposed to be someone for him, someone he'd be able to share his feelings with, someone who would share hers back, but

I wasn't like him and he was afraid I'd never want him, not like he wanted me and—

"Ben," I said, my voice breaking for him, aching for him, and when he heard that—when he heard me say his name, when he could sense what lay behind it—he dropped the bag he held and crossed to me so fast I didn't see it.

I just felt it, felt him pressed up against me, the two of us twining together, my back digging into the wall as his mouth touched mine, hesitantly at first and then deeper, harder.

Devouring.

Our feelings, our want, fed off each other, grew into something so strong and shining I half expected the air around us to shimmer.

I slid a hand up under his shirt, touching his stomach, the ridged muscles there, and then higher, over his chest. He groaned, whispered, "Avery," and I slid my hand lower, down to his waist, and then up across his back. I slid my fingers into the tiny patch that lay there, the proof of what he was, that he was more than human, and I thought—

I thought he was beautiful. I thought he was perfect for me.

I touched him and he touched me—mouths, hands— and then he trailed his mouth down my neck, circled it over my collarbone, pushing my shirt away as his hands

slid up under it, stroking the skin of my waist slowly, moving upward. I arched toward him, wanting him to move faster, wanting him, and he shook, he needed me so badly, and I heard a noise, a low, soft whimper, an animal sound of pure need.

But Ben didn't make it.

I did.

I did, and as I did Ben shivered, whispered my name and pressed in closer to me, sliding one hand down to hold my hips and I clung to him, wanting him, wanting—

"Uh, Avery?" I heard, and it wasn't Ben.

It was Renee.

My eyes flew open and I saw her standing right there, staring at Ben and me.

"I . . . Hi," I said.

She cleared her throat and said, "You said you were going to the bathroom."

"I ran into Ben."

Renee stared at us, unsmiling, and said, "I see that."

Ben drew away, shoving his hands into his pockets and dipping his head, submissive to Renee's clear anger. "I wasn't going to—"

"I think you'd better stop that sentence," Renee said. "I don't want to think about what would have happened if I hadn't come along. You're both only seventeen and clearly neither of you are thinking about what could happen, and Avery has been through enough." She

stared at Ben, her eyes narrowed. "Do you understand me?"

"I'd never hurt her," Ben said, his voice soft and solemn, and Renee looked at him.

"Then you're fine with leaving and letting her finish her dinner?" she said.

Ben swallowed, glancing at me, and I wanted—

Well, what I wanted made my toes curl.

But Ben only said, "Yes," and stepped away from me, picked up the bag he'd dropped.

"Good," Renee said, and looked right at him. "Tell Louis I said it was . . . interesting to meet his family."

"I—Avery," he said, looking at me.

Renee cleared her throat again and said, "I'm sure you need to get your dinner home. Right?"

Ben nodded, glanced at me, and then disappeared into the night, gone in a flash. Too fast to be human.

Renee didn't notice. She was too busy looking at me as I rearranged my shirt, ran my fingers over my kiss-swollen mouth.

"I think we need to go home," she said, and so we did.

She didn't say a word until we were almost at her house.

"I didn't know you liked Ben," she said.

"I—it's complicated," I said.

"Complicated?"

"Yes," I said softly. "I've never felt anything like what I do when I'm with him."

"Well, that isn't a surprise. You're young. I know, you don't want to hear that, but you are. You'll meet lots of boys and they'll . . . you'll feel like that with them too."

"No," I said. "I won't."

Renee blew out a breath at that, but she didn't say anything.

"Tell me what we'll do tomorrow," I said after we'd both been quiet for a moment. "Tell me about what's next for the porch."

"Avery, if you ever need to talk, I'm here, and I'll listen," she said, and then she did tell me about the porch.

As she talked, I looked over at her, at the worried set of her jaw, and wished I could tell her everything would be all right. That Ben and I were different, that we were nothing like ordinary.

I wanted to tell her that together we could do anything and that I knew it, heart and soul deep. I wanted to tell her that I trusted him and tonight had shown me I was right to do it.

But I didn't think that was what she wanted to hear, not now, so I just listened. I tried to think about what she said, and I did think about how we were still starting to get to know each other. She was starting to feel like family to me and I needed that, longed for it.

But I still thought about Ben, and hoped he thought of me.

Or I did, until I woke up the next morning and found out three people had been killed.

twenty-five

I didn't know what had happened when I first woke up. I'd been dreaming about Ben, about the two of us, and woke up blushing and glad no one could see into my dreams. Ben might be able to feel them though, and I wondered about that as I walked to the bathroom, tried to feel what he was feeling.

Nothing. I let out a little of what I'd seen in my dreams, let it flow into my mind, and tried to feel him again.

Still nothing. It was like he wasn't there at all.

And then I walked into the bathroom and saw my hair. The piece that I'd cut off, the blood red piece that had appeared overnight before—the one that had gotten me called cursed and made me feel like I was—it was back, shining stronger and darker than ever.

Shining like blood.

I swallowed, my head swimming, and rested my hands on the sink, leaning down over it. The strand fell into it, red against the white porcelain. I touched it, terrified it would feel wet. Sticky.

It didn't, but it was there. Blood red and shining, and I knew something had happened. Something horrible.

I just didn't know how horrible it really was.

When I went downstairs, Renee was already awake, standing in the kitchen staring at the kitchen table, her eyes red and swollen. She looked up when I came in.

She saw my hair even though I tried to tuck it away, and her face went pale.

"Avery, your . . . your hair," she said, stammering.

"The streak came back," I said. "I cut it off before, but it came back. It was there when I woke up. It came back, and I need you to tell me what's happened because I know something has."

She nodded, sitting down heavily in a kitchen chair, staring at the table again.

And then she told me.

Last night, in the light of the full moon, three people—the Thantos family—the whole family, Wallace and Kimberly and their daughter, Jane, had been killed.

"What?" I said, the strand of hair falling across my face, and Renee pushed the paper across the kitchen table to me.

I touched the strand as I read the article, which had

clearly been hastily written by the paper's one other employee, the woman who had laid out the articles for printing but now was writing too.

The Thantos family was dead, found just outside their home. They'd lived in the forest and not the town itself, just like me and Mom and Dad had. I'd seen them once in a while in town, but most often in the woods. They all walked through the trees like I did, with swift, sure strides.

They knew the woods. They knew how to be safe in them.

And yet all of them had died there. All of them had been murdered.

Worse, all of them had their throats ripped out. It was like they'd been killed by animals.

No, I told myself. *That isn't possible.* But then I thought of Mom and Dad and what had happened to them, and I put the paper down. I couldn't read anymore.

"Do the police know who did this? Have you heard from Ron? Whoever did this killed Mom and Dad too, I know it."

Renee shook her head. "What," she said. "What did this. They think it was an animal. A wolf. That it's sick. Rabid, or something."

I swallowed, my mouth suddenly dry, and Renee folded her hands together, said, "I see your hair, and I'm afraid for you. I don't believe in signs, but even I can't

ignore this. You must have seen something when your parents—" She broke off, her voice cracking.

"Or I'm tied to the forest somehow," I said, thinking of what Louis had said. Of my supposed power.

Was this it? To know death? To have it show up on me? To have it become part of me?

"That's not possible," Renee said, her voice shaking. "You can't be tied to a place, not even these woods. You live somewhere and that's all. But I am . . . I am worried about what all this is doing to you."

"I already know I don't remember what happened to my parents, believe me," I whispered, and she looked at me and said, "Oh, no, not that. I know you don't remember, but, honey, I'm worried about *you*, worried about how much stress you've been through."

"You really think an animal—a wolf—killed the Thantos family and my parents?" I said, my voice cracking.

"I don't know why a wolf would, but if it was rabid, I suppose it might happen. And they found wolf footprints out in the woods near the Thantos home," Renee said.

I needed to feel Ben more than I ever had now, needed to know that our trust—our bond—was real.

I still couldn't sense a thing.

I tried again, but my mind stayed blank. Empty of all feelings but my own. I didn't ask Renee if she was sure about the wolf prints that had been found. I could tell

she was, just like I knew my strange piece of hair had come back for a reason. It was a sign.

It meant something I didn't understand at all, and I was afraid Louis was right, that I was tied to the forest, and in a way that would always leave me surrounded by death.

Ben, please, I thought, brokenly, so broken, and closed my eyes.

"Avery?" Renee said. "I didn't know you knew the Thantos family that well. I guess I should have, since they lived out in the forest too. Should I call someone? Ron, maybe? Would that help?"

"No," I said softly, and then again, louder, opening my eyes.

I didn't need someone watching me. I needed to remember what had happened to my parents, and I needed to do it now. The only problem was, I needed to find a way to do it. It shouldn't have been so hard, but no matter what I did, no matter what I'd tried, I couldn't see what had happened. But I knew, deep down, that I had seen it all.

So why was it so hidden inside my head?

I was afraid I knew. In spite of what I felt for Ben, in spite of how my heart longed for him, I was terrified of what would happen when I did remember. I was terrified of what I'd see, of what that gleaming silver I did remember would turn out to be.

Wolf.

I couldn't—wouldn't—think past that. Not now. I touched the strand of hair again, my heart contracting, aching.

Renee got up and said, "Let me get you something to eat."

I shook my head. "I need to be alone for a little while," I said, and went back up to the guest room that was my room. I crawled into bed and cried for the Thantos family, for my parents, and for myself.

I cried because everything was broken and I didn't know what to do.

twenty-six

I went to the church service for the Thantos family with Renee. My eyes were red, but then so were everyone else's, and the service was quiet, a few general prayers but mostly people sharing what they knew about the Thantos family.

There wasn't much. The Thantos family was nice enough, but they'd been quiet and kept to themselves. Came to town very rarely. Had a daughter who'd gone to Woodlake High for a little while, graduated, and then stayed in the woods with her parents.

"Jane was at home in the woods," one person said. "They were part of her," and it hit me that this service could have been my family's memorial service. If things had been just a little different—if Mom hadn't sent me out for mushrooms—what had just been said could have easily been about me.

There was only one difference, really.

Jane had died.

I hadn't.

I felt the strand of hair fall free from where I'd tucked it behind my ear then, and I touched it. If the forest had given me some sort of power, I wished that it could be used to stop what had happened. To stop all this death.

I didn't want to be part of this, and yet I was.

We prayed for the Thantos family again after everyone was done speaking, asked God to watch over their souls.

"We ask for your grace and mercy," the minister said. "We ask that you watch over everyone in Woodlake, that you guide those who need you. We ask that you watch over all of God's creatures."

I'd had my head bowed, but I looked up when he said that and saw the minister had his eyes open.

He was looking at Louis, who had come in and was sitting in the back of the church, silent and alone.

As the last hymn finished playing, I got up and walked toward Louis. I heard Renee say, "Avery?" as I did, but I didn't turn back because I had to see him.

I had to know why Louis was here, and I had to know what he knew about the Thantos family and their deaths.

I wanted to know what he knew about my so-called power.

But when I got to the back of the church, he was gone.

I pushed through the small crowd standing crying by the door. I heard them murmur my name as I said, "Excuse me," and "I'm sorry," trying to get through. I didn't *feel* what they wanted to know, not like I could with Ben, but I still knew what they wanted anyway.

They wanted to know why I had lived when everyone else attacked in the woods died. They wanted to know what I knew about everything that had happened.

They wondered what I knew. What I'd done.

That last thought stopped me cold. In all my dreams and imaginings, in all that I'd seen and wondered, I hadn't ever thought—

I hadn't ever thought of what my lack of memory could mean for me. How the gleaming silver could have been just a trick of my mind. A way to make me think that someone else had done horrible things when maybe the person who had was . . . me?

Could I have done that? Had I done that?

No. My mind recoiled like I'd been hit, and not gently. I felt the pull of my hair, that changed strand, and it didn't say I was the one who had done this.

It just said—without words, in a way that just washed over me, through me—that I was the one who knew what had happened.

I stepped outside the church.

Louis was already out in the parking lot, walking toward the cemetery and the woods that lay at the end of it.

I ran after him.

He must have heard me coming because he stopped and turned, waiting.

"Avery," he said right before I reached him, and I stopped short, so many questions racing through my mind that I suddenly had no idea where to begin.

"I knew the Thantos family," Louis said after a moment, his voice gentle. "They were good people. Kind. Loved the forest. I haven't been close enough to where it . . . to where it all happened to be sure, but I think that whoever killed your parents also killed them. I think you should go back to your grandmother and stay in her house. Stay out of the woods."

"What about my power?" I said, and pulled out the piece of hair that had changed color again. Louis stared at it. "Is . . . is my power death?"

"No," Louis said. "The forest feels its losses—not like a human would, but it does feel them—and it's chosen to show those losses through you. I didn't—" His voice was shaking. "I didn't think this could ever happen again. I thought it ended the last time. Hide your hair, Avery. Hide it from everyone."

"Even Renee?"

"No," he said again. "Not from her. She's family, she'll understand. I have to go now, all right? But you really do need to stay out of the woods. Don't even go in them for Ben."

"You still don't want me to see him?"

"Yes," Louis said, one word. Simple, direct, and it broke me more. "He is . . . confused now."

"What? Why?" I said, but Louis didn't answer me, just vanished into the trees, moving faster than any human could. But then, Louis wasn't totally human either, just like Ben.

Louis was part wolf.

Louis could have—

No, Louis hadn't killed my parents. He hadn't killed me, and he could have any time, even just now, but instead he'd told me what my so-called power was.

The forest knew everything that happened in it. I'd known that, of course, on some distant level, in an of-course-it-does-because-it's-nature way, but I hadn't realized the forest could—well, that it could *feel*.

But it did, in its own strange, ancient, and inhuman way, a way I didn't understand, and it had chosen me to hold its rhythms, its waitings. Its changes—those known and unknown.

No, Louis wasn't a killer. He hadn't done anything but help me. He didn't want me in the woods, though, but that was because of Ben.

But what if, in forgetting my parents' murders, I'd forgotten something else too? And what if the forest was trying to tell me something in its own way? I touched my hair again then, thinking about what Ben had said

last night. About how I was like a myth. How I saw things that other people couldn't.

"Avery?" Renee said behind me, and I jumped so hard my teeth clacked together. "What are you doing out here?"

"I . . . Mom and Dad," I said.

Renee looked at me for a moment, and then led me over to their graves.

She didn't ask why I hadn't gone straight to them, and when we reached them I forgot everything and sank to my knees.

I hadn't seen the graves since the earth was freshly turned over and my parents had been put in it forever. I looked at the ground, slowly smoothing out now, the raw earth fading away.

I looked at the headstones, at their names. At the dates.

They ended too soon, far too soon.

I looked at the tree that had been carved at the bottom of each stone, a sign of what my parents loved.

Had that love somehow killed them?

I knelt and put a hand on each grave. I waited to feel something, but I just felt earth, cool under my hand. I didn't feel my parents with me; I didn't feel them watching over me. I still didn't know what or who had taken them from me.

I thought of Louis, sitting in the back of the church, and what the minister had said about all of God's

creatures. I wondered if there were other people in town who knew what I did. Were there others who thought of the wolves and the woods and asked themselves if there was something different about it all? Did they think about the story of how Woodlake was founded and believe there was truth in it? Did they wonder about the wolves that still lived in its forest?

"How well do you know Louis?" I said to Renee, looking over my shoulder at her.

She was staring down at my parents' grave but she froze when I spoke, stood perfectly still, her face looking shattered.

"I used to know him," she finally said. "We went to school together for a little while—high school, actually. But that was a long time ago. I haven't spoken to him in years. Haven't seen him in years."

"Is he—?" I swallowed. "Does he seem . . . different to you?"

"No different than anyone else who spends his whole life in the woods," Renee said, but she didn't look at me as she said it.

She knew. What exactly she knew, I couldn't tell. But she knew something, just like the minister had.

I took a deep breath. "Could he have killed the Thantos family? Killed Mom and Dad?"

"No," Renee said, looking startled. "Louis would never do anything like that. No one from around here is doing

this. No one in Woodlake has a heart this evil. Ron is bringing in someone from the FBI to help out with the case because it supposedly fits a profile of other killings."

"There have been other killings? Deaths exactly like Mom and Dad's? Like the Thantos family?"

Renee looked at me for a long moment and then she nodded. "That's what I've heard. And as for the FBI, well, Ron wouldn't bring them in unless he had reason to." She turned to me.

"I saw you in the church today," she said, her voice soft. "When everyone spoke about the Thantos family you thought the same thing I did, and Avery, all those things they said about Jane could have been said about you. I think we . . ." She took a deep breath. "I have a little money saved, and I think that you and I should take a vacation. In fact, I think we should go away—far away—now."

"Away? Now?"

"Yes. I have to make arrangements, but we'll leave tomorrow," Renee said. "You won't even need to go to school. You can just stay home and pack today, and then tomorrow morning we'll drive to the airport. I don't think you should leave the house at all, actually. Not unless I'm with you. Okay?"

"I . . . all right," I said, stunned. "But where are we going?"

"It's a surprise," she said, and I looked at her. Saw the worried lines on her face.

"You think I'll tell someone who shouldn't know," I said. "Who?"

"There are some people who have a way of getting you to say things you don't mean to say," Renee said softy. "Of getting to the truth in your heart, and I want—need—you to be safe. That's why I don't want you going out until we leave. Now let's go home and I'll make us something to eat and you can sand some wood for the porch while I make a few phone calls to set everything up."

"It's not like that with Ben," I said, knowing exactly who she was talking about, and I was right because she didn't say anything, just closed her eyes, briefly, and then looked at me.

"How long have you known Ben?"

"Not long," I said. "But we—"

"I know," she said. "I saw you two last night, and I know you feel something for him, but sometimes people say things and suddenly that becomes all you can think about. They can be all you can think about. You're vulnerable now, hurting because of what's happened to you, and I don't want to see you hurt more. So, yes, when I say no going out, I mean no seeing Ben."

"But he would never hurt me, and besides, he can't make me say things I don't want to or do things I don't want to. We—" I broke off then because what was I going to say? That I could sense Ben's thoughts and he could sense mine? That he'd tried to do exactly what Renee had

just suggested—that he'd tried to talk me into staying out of the woods—and that it hadn't worked? That, for whatever reason, any abilities he and Louis had to make people think or do things didn't seem to work on me at all? That Ben agreed with Renee about me being tied to all of this?

Just thinking it sounded crazy. I was just a girl, a normal, nothing girl, a girl who had seen her life shatter and—

And the blood red strand of hair fell free again and swung across my face, curved around my jaw, the ends trailing up toward my lips.

It couldn't have smelled like blood.

But it did, and now I was almost positive I knew what it meant. The forest was grieving.

I shivered, and Renee said, "Let's go," gently, so gently, and we went back to the church. Ron waved us over in the parking lot as we headed for the car.

"Hey there," he called and then stopped, staring as he saw my hair.

"You—Avery, what's going on with you?" he said, his eyes wide, and I didn't want to upset him. He'd already seen so much death, had already watched over me when I was too broken to even move. He'd been there to help me as I'd sat, blood-soaked, beside what was left of my parents.

"Hair dye gone bad," I said, trying to make my voice

light. "I was trying to put streaks in but instead I ended up with this." I tucked the blood red piece behind my ear, pushing it out of sight. "The worst thing is, I have to wait a day before I can dye it back."

I had no idea if that was true or not, but Ron seemed happier when I said it. He relaxed a little then, smiled at Renee, and said, "Back when we were young, I bet that's one thing John never did try to drive you crazy."

Renee laughed. It was strained-sounding, but it was still a laugh, and I wished Dad could have seen how much Renee loved him. I wished they had been able to talk when there—when there was still time.

"No, he never did dye his hair. Although you and he both needed haircuts all through high school."

"No, not me," Ron said, smiling back at her, and then glanced at me. "I . . . Avery, I know this is hard, but when you heard what happened to the Thantos family, did it make you remember anything more? Anything at all?"

Nothing new. Just Mom urging me to go outside and get mushrooms. Just that and silver.

Silver, bright silver, inhuman in how fast it moved, how angry it seemed . . .

How angry it was.

"No," I said. "I've tried but I . . ." I trailed off, ashamed of how I'd failed.

"It's all right," Ron said. "I know how you were when I came and got you. The FBI agent asked about you first

thing—as if you were a suspect!—but I set him straight. You're a victim, Avery, and I know that. I want you to understand I'll do everything I can to look out for you. To take care of you."

"Thank you," I said, and he nodded, then tipped his hat at Renee and walked off, heading for his car. He passed Steve on the way and nodded at him too.

As soon as I realized Steve was coming toward us, I tensed.

"Let's go," I whispered, my skin prickling.

"Renee," Steve called out and I sighed, causing Steve to glance at me before he grinned at Renee and walked over to us. To her.

"I just came over to ask you to please think about my offer again," he said. "I'll still pay what I offered even though it seems the woods are becoming a place of death."

He stuck his hands in his pockets. "I don't think John would want you to hold on to that land now. He always wanted the woods to be full of life, and just—think about that, all right? Promise me you will."

"I will," Renee said, and Steve smiled.

"Call me anytime you want to talk," he said, and then walked over to his car.

As soon as he was gone, I turned to her. "You can't sell the woods!"

"Avery, the house is gone—I can't stop that from

being destroyed at all, and your father . . . first his death and your mother's, and now another family's?" Renee said. "You think he'd want that legacy for you? That he'd want me to hold on to that for you? That he'd even want you in the forest now?"

"He would."

"No, he wouldn't. He'd want you to be safe. He loved you more than he loved the woods."

"Don't sell the woods. The forest belongs only to itself," I said, and there was something strange in my voice, something commanding. It seemed to come from somewhere deep inside me, from a place I didn't know I had, and as I finished speaking I realized it came from the woods.

The forest really did experience what happened in it, not like a human did, but in a deeper way, a way that went past time as I or anyone else knew it, and I was its voice now.

I was its imperfect, human voice.

I really had been chosen, and everything Louis had said was right. The strand in my hair meant that I had power. I could feel it now. It was there, waiting, in the rawness I sensed beyond my parents' death and my worry over Ben.

The forest was trying to speak through me.

It *had* spoken through me.

Renee blinked at me slowly, her eyes blank in a way I'd never seen before.

"I won't sell," she said, her voice so even and flat it made my skin prickle, and then she shook her head and said, "I don't even know why I thought about it, but you're right. I can't sell the land, and especially not to Steve, who'd just tear everything down and get rid of the trees your parents loved so much. Come on, we need to get back to the house."

She sounded normal then, she sounded like herself, and I was almost able to forget what had happened.

Almost, because the hair that I'd cut away had come back again, and on the way home it swung free once more, falling across my face.

When it touched my lips, it tasted metallic and dark.

It tasted like blood, and I remembered the three people who'd died last night. I felt how the forest mourned them and everything that had happened.

I couldn't hear the tone in Ben's or Louis's voices that was supposed to make me want to listen, to obey, but I'd just made Renee agree to something when she'd been thinking about doing the exact opposite. I wasn't like Ben, but yet—

I looked into the woods as we pulled into the driveway.

The forest had claimed me somehow. Changed me.

It needed me, but what did the woods want me to know? To do? Why had they picked me?

And if the woods could do so much, then why had they let my parents be murdered?

I looked at them once more, but they were silent. They had no answers for me.

None that I could hear, anyway. I just felt fear.

My own, and more.

It wasn't Ben's. It came from something strange and old, something that had been here since before men ever were.

It came from the forest, and the feeling I had was nothing like with Ben, nothing so strong and sure, but instead was just a low, steady whisper. A skittering, scared breath that only I could hear.

That only I could help.

twenty-seven

Renee definitely didn't want me going anywhere and so she had me help her make lunch, and then, while she made phone calls, I sat and sanded a big piece of wood at the kitchen table. I used sandpaper, just like Dad had always done when he was building something, the wood slowly softening, with only a few faint curls falling to show progress.

I was sitting looking out at where the porch was going to be, and I could see into the forest.

I could see into the forest, but Renee could see me. She smiled whenever I glanced over my shoulder at her, as if she was reminding me to stay where I was.

As if she knew the forest was calling me.

The forest wasn't, though. I didn't feel like I *had* to walk through it or be in it. I just wanted to because it was where I'd always gone when I was upset, when I needed to think. It was what my parents had done, and they'd taught me to do it too.

They weren't in the forest anymore, though. Now they lay in a churchyard free of trees. They were in the ground, under soil the forest hadn't touched in years.

What had happened after Mom asked me to get mushrooms? Why weren't any with me when I was found? Where had I been? What had I seen?

I always picked mushrooms for Mom by putting them into a little tan bag she'd made, one that almost matched the color of the forest floor. It had fit around my waist when I was little but as I got older I'd tied it to a belt loop on my pants or just wrapped it around one wrist.

If it had fallen and the trees had blown leaves over it, no one would have spotted it. It could still be there, and if I found it—

If I found it, I would know where I was when everything happened.

And if I knew that, then maybe more would come back to me. Maybe then I'd finally remember all of that night.

I wanted that, but I also wanted to see Ben too. I closed my eyes, thought of him, and felt . . .

I could only feel worry. Deep, endless worry. I felt him try to push it away, but it wouldn't go.

Something was wrong. I needed to see him and waited for him to feel that, waited for him to react like he always

198 • Ivy Devlin

did, with feelings that made me believe I was beautiful and needed.

But that wasn't what he thought.

Instead, he panicked.

He didn't want to see me, he didn't want me coming into the woods, not now, not after—

Everything went quiet then.

Everything shifted, and the panic became something deeper, more primal.

Ben had . . .

He had changed. I wondered why for a moment, and then I knew. He'd changed because he was afraid. Because I had felt his fear, and something about that, about me, scared him.

I thought of what he'd said about the full moon and how, if he'd changed last night, he wouldn't have been able to change back until sunrise.

I had to see him now. I had to talk to him.

I also had to find the mushroom bag.

I turned the piece of wood I was holding over and rubbed the sandpaper across it again. I glanced at Renee, who wasn't looking at me any longer. Instead, she was looking out into the woods, a frown on her face as she kept talking on the phone in a low voice.

I didn't ask to go out because I knew she'd say no. I also knew that if I tried to leave at night she would be up, waiting for me. She already knew I'd left the house at night before, and she had seen Ben and me together.

She had already told me she didn't want me to see him again.

When she was done on the phone, I asked her where we were going.

"It's a surprise."

I nodded then, like everything was fine, like it wasn't strange that she wouldn't tell me, and said, "Could I—would it be all right if I packed now? I'd like to be busy. To not think about things."

Renee came over and took my hands in hers. "Of course. I—about where we're going, I want it to be a surprise because I don't want you to . . . I want you to be safe. Do you understand?"

No.

But I didn't say that. Instead I said, "Dad used to sand wood just like this," and smiled at her.

She smiled back. "I know. How about I take over and you can go start to pack? I'll come check on you in a little bit."

I nodded again. "I'll leave my door open so I can hear you if you need anything or whatever."

"Great," Renee said, and as soon as she did, I said, "Wait. I don't have a suitcase. There's one at the house, but Ron brought . . . everything came in boxes."

"I have an extra one in the attic," Renee said. "Just give me fifteen minutes to find it."

"Okay," I said, and helped her open the door that led up to the attic, watched as she walked up the steps into it.

And then, when she was up inside the very top of the house looking for a suitcase for me, I went downstairs, moving quietly. Quickly.

I went outside. I didn't go into the backyard. There was a window in the attic and it looked out onto the woods. Renee would be glancing out it, I knew that, and I—

Well, I needed the head start. I needed time to get into the woods.

To get to where most people didn't go.

So instead of crossing her backyard, I walked down her street, all the way down to the end, and skirted around the house that sat there, empty, with a big STEVE BROWNING PROPERTIES sign plastered across it, and then headed into the woods.

Renee would be upset, but even if she sent Ron and the whole police force after me, they wouldn't find me. Not where I was going.

I wasn't going back to my house. I wasn't even going to look for my mushroom bag. At least, not yet.

I was looking for Ben.

I walked into the woods and thought of him. I thought only of him and I didn't wonder where I was walking, didn't look at the trees I passed by.

I walked, and I let my heart guide me.

I ended up deep in the forest, the trees so tall above me I felt as tiny and new as they must have seen me.

I walked, and deep in the forest, in a place I knew I'd

never been before, I found Ben. He was sitting beside one of those tall old trees, his head in his hands.

His feet were bare and smudged with dirt, like he'd been running.

"Avery," he said as I walked toward him, and of course he knew I was coming, that I'd find him. That was how things were between us.

He looked like the forest, beautiful and inhuman. He looked like Ben, and he looked so alone that I went straight to him, sat down and rested my head on his shoulder, breathing in the warm forest scent of him.

He turned and pulled me to him, his fingers touching my hair. Freezing when they found the blood red strand.

"This—"

"It was there when I woke up this morning."

He was silent for a moment.

"I don't remember last night," he said. "After I saw you I was so…" He paused. "I wanted you so much I almost came to you. I wanted to come to your grandmother's house and find you, climb into the house and touch you—"

My breath caught at what he was feeling, my mind creating images of opening my eyes to see Ben in front of me. Ben in the room that was mine now. Ben by my bed, on it, in it. I moved a little closer to him then, my breath coming faster, and Ben let out a low cry and pushed away from me.

"I changed," he said, and the words sounded like they

were ripped from him. "I—I needed you so much I scared myself and I changed so I wouldn't come to you."

"You changed? But you said if you changed last night, you couldn't change back until the morning, that all night you'd be a wol—" I broke off, thinking of what had happened last night. How the Thantos family had died, their throats all ripped out like an animal had attacked them.

A wolf, the paper and Renee had said.

A wolf.

"Ben, you really don't remember anything?" I whispered, and he didn't move, stayed where he was.

Didn't look at me.

twenty-eight

Ben," I said again and he shook his head and said, "I don't remember, but I didn't hurt the Thantos family— I would never do anything like that. Not ever."

"There must be something you can remember," I said. "I've felt your feelings when you're ... when you're not human, and they're different but you still have them, so a part of you must still be there. Still see what happens."

Ben said, "Avery, please," but I sensed what he felt.

Fear.

He couldn't stop it, and last night he'd been afraid as well. I sensed all of that, felt it, and knew he'd run as deep into the woods as he could, desperate and long- ing for something that part of him—the animal part— couldn't name.

And then everything shifted, turned. Became about the hunt and there had been running. Prey, and a chase, then the simple joy of taking it down.

"No," I whispered, my skin prickling with goose bumps.

"It's part of who I am," Ben said, low-voiced. "I was out here, but I was in this part of the woods, and no one lives here. Whenever I change, I go out into the woods as far as I can. I go to where no humans are. I go to where I won't be seen because I can't afford to be."

"Then what did you hunt? What did you *kill*?"

"An animal. I don't remember what kind. I woke up and there weren't any bo—whatever it was, it was gone." He swallowed.

"You eat . . . everything?" I thought of bones crunching between his teeth and felt sick.

"No, when I done, when I'm full, I move on," he said. "Look, I swear that whatever it was couldn't have been human. No human ever comes out here."

"I'm here."

"Avery, you're a little more than human too." He looked at my hair. "I can feel the forest in you, actually, and it knows so much more than I do. More than I understand."

I closed my eyes, but the forest was silent. Still. It was as if it was waiting, as if I needed to keep going, to keep asking questions I didn't want to.

I took a deep breath and turned away. It was easier to ask what I needed to when I didn't have to look at him.

"Ben, when you woke up, are you sure you didn't see anything? There was no sign of what you hunted at all?"

"No."

"Was there blood on you?"

"I—"

"Was there?" My voice cracked.

"Yes, on my hands," he said softly, and I looked at him then.

"How did it get there?" I said, and now he looked away from me. He also didn't answer, but then he didn't have to. I could tell he didn't know.

He didn't remember what—or worse, who—he'd hunted.

My heart was beating so hard I could feel it. I heard the trees above me sway as if they had a heart that beat in tandem with mine, their leaves trembling.

"Ben, where were you when my parents were killed?"

"I wasn't anywhere. I'd just come to town."

"You didn't go out at all?"

"I walked through the forest some," he said slowly, so slowly.

"Did you change?"

"Avery," he whispered, and I remembered the soft silver mark of the wolf that lived inside him.

I knew what the answer was.

"You did, didn't you?" I said, my voice shaking, and he nodded and then got up and crossed over to me, grabbing my arms when I started to move farther away, his eyes brown and pleading.

"I know I didn't hurt your family or anyone else," he

said. "After what happened to my family, how could I? I know what I am, and I'm not a killer."

"But you don't remember last night."

"I was here," he said. "I know that. And I know there aren't any people out here. There's never any people out here!"

"Except for me, now."

"Avery—"

"What if I had been here last night?"

"You're here now because you felt my emotions and because you decided you had to find me," he said. "Last night you wouldn't have been able to, and even if you had, I'd know you. Even as a—"

"A wolf?"

"Yes," he said, his jaw tight—with anger? Fear? I couldn't tell, his emotions were so tangled—and I thought of Renee, of the vacation she'd planned, of going away, and Ben stiffened.

"Away?" he said. "You're leaving?"

I looked at him.

"Yes," I said. "I am."

His hands gripped me harder then, his eyes flashing, shifting from brown to silver, from human to inhuman, and he whispered, "I won't be able to feel you, and I need that. I need—"

Me.

He needed me, and his thoughts were full of want, of

wishing he'd come to me last night instead of running off. And under that, beside it, was fear. Fear that I'd never come back. That he'd lose me. That all he'd have left were memories of me, of how I looked, smelled. Tasted. How I'd craved him that night in my parents' house, in the woods, and then last night.

"Wait," I said. I'd realized a way I could know for sure that Ben, despite having forgotten last night, wasn't a killer.

I told him about the mushroom bag, about how I'd had it with me, and how it had disappeared.

"I think that if I find it, I might remember what happened. And if I can do that, then all of this will be over. Will you help me look for it? We could find it together and then—" I broke off as I sensed panic, bone-deep, soul-deep panic, sweep over him.

"What is it?"

But as soon as I said it, I knew. I could almost taste his guilt.

"You found it," I said. *"You?"*

"I went out in the woods my first night here. Everything I'd known was gone and Louis was—he's nice, but I didn't know him. I just needed to get out. So I did. And . . ."

I knew what his pause meant. "You changed."

He nodded. "Afterward, I found a bag, a little one, lying on the ground."

"Near my house?"

He shifted a little. "Sort of. It was just lying there, and it . . . it looked homemade. It made me think about my family. About what I'd lost. I kept it, actually."

I was shaking now. "Did it have mushrooms in it?"

"A few," he said slowly, and I thought of the last thing my mother had asked me to do. The last thing I remembered doing, and how the bag, when I'd finally come back to the world, to the horror that lay before me, was gone.

It was gone because Ben had it.

Ben had "found" it.

It had made him think about what he'd lost. So there he'd been, alone and sad.

Angry.

He'd been there.

"No," I said, my eyes filling with tears as I backed away from him, shaking all over. "You were here in Woodlake when my parents died. You were here, and you weren't— you *changed*. You were upset, you weren't human, and then *you* found my bag. You were right there when it all happened. When my parents died. You—"

"No," he said, shaking his head. "No, that can't be. I found that bag after I changed back and it was sort of close to your house, but I'm sure I didn't—"

"Are you?" I said, and stared right at him because I could feel his worry.

He wasn't sure.

"I've never hurt anyone," he said. "I found your bag, I did, and last night I changed, but I came out here."

"Because you don't know if you can keep the part of you that isn't human away when you're around me, right? What about someone else? Would you care then?"

"Yes, and it's not that simple!" he said. "It's not like it sounds. I would know you anywhere. You *know* that."

"But not my parents. Not the Thantos family."

"Stop it," he said, and kissed me then, holding me tight. He needed me, wanted all of me, wanted me forever. I had run when I'd first found out what he was, but I'd come back and he'd hoped even as he told himself not to.

And then I'd told him I'd trusted him. I'd said that, and I was here now. I cared. He could feel that.

But then he sensed what lay under that. What I was afraid to say.

What I thought he might have done.

What he couldn't remember. And I felt his worry again. His *what if*—?

He didn't know. He wondered.

I broke away from him, taking a step back.

"Avery," he whispered, and his eyes looked into mine, so full of feeling, so—

So silver.

Noise.

There had been noise that night, the night my parents died, and I'd heard it. I remembered now, I could hear it right now, and I—

I was crouching behind a tree, hidden by it with one hand pressed to my mouth so I wouldn't scream as I saw silver flash, and a terrible sound, the sound of flesh ripping, tearing apart, filled the air. I could hear my father moaning, my mother screaming, and I closed my eyes but knew the silver was still there. I heard it as it flashed and struck over and over again, and it didn't stop until there was total silence. Wrong silence. And that was when I crept out, when the blood began to pool around me. To cover me.

"No," I said, and scrambled away from Ben, from the memory.

I couldn't forget either, though, and I couldn't stop seeing it.

I'd been there that night, and now I realized what had happened. I'd seen that silver moving, gleaming, shifting. It had torn into my parents, silver and red blood everywhere, and it wasn't human, nothing human moved like that, nothing destroyed like that and—

Silver.

Ben, with his silver eyes.

Ben, who wasn't totally human.

Ben, who couldn't remember that night.

"Avery," he whispered, but no, I wasn't going to hear him now. I couldn't.

I looked at him, and made myself think of the pattern that had been on his back the first night we kissed, and how shocked I'd been. I made myself think of what my father had taught me about wolves. How it was important to respect them. To let them be.

He should have taught me one more thing. He should have taught me to realize they hunted, and to never, ever forget that.

No, my heart screamed. *No, no, no, no.*

But the bag, and Ben's anger that first night, the night my parents died—it all made so much sense, made horrible, true sense. His family, dead, and him so furious.

Changed.

I took a slow step back, my eyes burning, my heart pounding in sorrow and in fear.

"Avery, please," Ben said, but I didn't stop moving. I couldn't. I wouldn't.

"I love you," he called out, his voice breaking.

I stopped then.

"I love you," he said again, and I froze because I knew he meant it.

He truly did love me … but he couldn't remember last night. Or the night my parents died. It was all a blur of animal sensation, of feelings that I couldn't reach. That he was—

That he was afraid to reach.

"I'm not a killer," he whispered, moving toward me

slowly, so slowly, giving me time to feel how much he loved me. To feel how much he believed what he said.

Or at least, how much he wanted to believe it.

"Stop," I said, the word coming out stronger than I ever knew I could be, and I knew the forest was flowing through me. It was immense, powerful beyond belief.

Ben stilled, his eyes huge. I watched him try to move, but he couldn't.

The forest held him because I wanted it to.

"Avery," he whispered once more but I turned around, turned away from him. I walked away slowly at first and then faster, faster, running.

I didn't look back.

Tears streamed down my face as I remembered my parents and how they'd died, and the forest grieved with me, grieved in a deep, brutal way that shook me. I didn't know if the woods felt rage, loss, fear, or all of it. I just knew that *I* did.

There was an endless scream trapped inside me, one that came straight from my heart, and I knew what— who—it was for. It was for Ben.

My heart beat for Ben, but I had to let that go. I had to.

But no matter how fast I ran, I still thought of him.

twenty-nine

I ran back to Renee's, forgetting that I'd left her up in the attic thinking I was waiting for a suitcase, forgetting that I'd lied to her. I remembered as soon as I ran in the house though, because she was sitting on the kitchen floor, crying like the world had ended.

That was how I wanted to cry.

"Avery!" she said when she saw me and I heard anger and terror and relief in her voice. I heard love.

"I—I," I said, and then I burst into tears.

She got up and came to me, folded her arms around me. Had I let her really hug me since my parents died? I couldn't remember.

She hugged me, held me tight, and I hugged her back, glad she was there. She always had been; I realized that now. When I was little, I'd loved her, and then I'd turned away. But my heart hadn't forgotten that love and I felt it now, felt it as I felt my grandmother hold me.

"Grandma," I said, and heard her breath hitch. "Something terrible happened and I—" I broke off. I couldn't bring myself to say Ben's name, or what I was so afraid was beyond horrible but true.

I didn't want to think it could have been Ben that ended my life as I knew it, but in spite of my untrustworthy heart, I had to speak because my parents deserved it. They shouldn't have died, and even if Ben loved me, even if I loved him—and I shouldn't, because how could I feel that way knowing what I did?—I had to say what I knew.

"Silver," I whispered, and Renee stared at me.

"What?" she said.

"I saw silver when Mom and Dad died," I said. The next words would be so hard to say, but I could do it. I *had* to do it.

"I saw . . . I saw something that wasn't human," I said. "I think what killed the Thantos family killed Mom and Dad, and I know the paper said it was a wolf, but I think—" I broke off.

I only had to say, "It was Ben." That was all, just three words, but they caught in my throat. They made my heart ache, and I couldn't say them after all.

I couldn't say those three words. Not even now.

"Silver?" Renee whispered. "You mean like wolves' eyes? Like a wolf that isn't always a wolf?"

I stared at her. How did she know about that?

"I've lived here almost my entire life," she said, as if she'd heard my unspoken question. "I've heard the stories. I know what lives in the woods."

"Dad didn't believe in them."

"I know," she said. "I raised him to believe they were just stories and nothing more because I had to. And now I have to know . . . Avery, what did you see?"

I told her.

I watched her face pale as I spoke of how I'd seen silver—inhuman, moving so fast, so violently—tearing into my parents. How I'd hidden and seen it all happen.

"And then when Ben . . . when Ben said he'd found my mushroom bag, the one I'd had with me because Mom had sent me out, I just . . . I knew what had happened."

"Oh, no," Renee said, her voice breaking, and she was crying again. "Are you sure Ben is—?"

"Yes," I whispered before she could finish her sentence. I couldn't bear to hear those last words, I wanted them left unsaid even as I knew what they were. "I don't want to be sure. But I am."

"But why would he want to hurt your parents?"

"His parents—his whole family—was killed, and I know he's upset about it. And when he changes, I don't know if he can control himself. He says he'd never hurt me, but he doesn't remember that night or last night, and this morning he woke up with blood on his hands."

Renee stared at me. "Who killed his parents?"

"He just said Hunters, people who want to kill people like . . . like him." My voice broke. "Is that true? Or was he—?" I couldn't bring myself to ask if he was lying.

"I've heard stories about Hunters who spend their lives trying to find people who are—who are more than human. And I know that if they do find them, they kill them."

"How do you know that?" I said, startled, but she shook her head and said, "I told you I've lived here almost my entire life. Ben isn't . . . there are others like him in the woods, and I used to—" She broke off, took a deep breath.

"We have to call Ron," she said. "We need him out here *now*. He'll be able to find Ben, and he'll send someone to watch over us, keep us safe."

"You can't," I whispered. "Renee, he loves me. And I . . ." I knew what came next. I *felt* it. But to say it in spite of everything—

What would that make me?

I waited for Renee's face to twist in anger or revulsion, but instead she knelt down next to me, cupped her hands around my face.

"He's powerful," she said. "They all are. Avery, they are beautiful, they are like nothing—no one else—and they can make you think forever is possible. They can make you believe anything."

"But he can't. That's the thing. He can't make me think what he wants me to. He tried, but it didn't work."

"What did he try to . . . what did he want you to do?" Renee said, her voice shaking. "Did you two—?"

"No," I said, shaking my head, but I knew heat crept into my face and didn't dare tell her that I'd wanted to do what she was thinking. "He just asked me to stay out of the woods."

"That's it?" Renee said, and I closed my eyes, sadness sweeping over me.

"He didn't want me to go into the house," I whispered. "I went out to see it but he—he stopped me."

He'd saved me from that falling tree.

Or had he?

"And you didn't go to the house, did you? Just like he wanted." Renee's voice was soft, understanding, and I shook my head, tears filling my eyes again.

My heart was full of emotion. Full of Ben. And I—

For my parents, I had to do this.

"Call Ron," I said. "Tell him I know who killed my parents." I swallowed. "Tell him . . . tell him about Ben and the bag."

thirty

I listened while Renee talked to Ron because she put the call on speakerphone. She sat next to me while she talked to him, an arm around me like she knew I needed it. I did.

Ron sucked in a breath when she told him what I'd remembered and said, "I'll send everyone out to look for Ben now, and I'll come over right away. Lock all the doors, all the windows, and no matter what, don't let anyone in. Do you understand?"

"Yes," Renee said.

"I mean it," Ron said. "After what happened to John and Debby and to the Thantos family—you can't trust anyone, Renee. No matter what someone might come to you and say, you don't listen. No matter how . . . persuasive they might be."

"You know about the wolves?" Renee said, surprise coloring her voice, and Ron said, "You too? I've suspected things about Woodlake and the forest for years. How could I not, with how it's always seemed to fight me? I guess I just didn't want it to be true, but now I need you to stay safe. Keep Avery safe. And remember, no one comes in but me. I'll be there as soon as I can."

He paused, then said, "And don't...don't let Avery out. No matter what happens, no matter what she says, you keep her with you. Don't let her listen to anyone but you or me."

"I will," Renee said, and hung up the phone.

We locked all the doors and windows—or Renee did while I followed her, her hand clutching mine, keeping me with her.

Renee even went back up into the attic to lock the tiny window that looked out onto the forest. "There, that's everything," she said. Her hands weren't shaking, but mine sure were.

As she clicked the lock into place, someone knocked on the front door.

My heart jumped, beating so fast I half expected to see it fly out of my chest, and as we went downstairs— Renee moving slowly, cautiously—I could only stare at the door, frozen. Scared.

Hoping.

In spite of everything, I still wanted to see Ben. I pressed my hands to my face, wishing I could be smarter, less bound to my own heart.

Renee whispered, "Go into the kitchen—no, the dining room," and went to the door.

I started toward the dining room but stopped and turned when I heard Renee suck in a breath. She was staring out the front door peephole, her hands resting in fists on the door.

"You're in danger," someone said.

It was Louis.

Louis? Did he know—had he known about Ben?

I ran toward the door and cried, "Why didn't you tell me about Ben? Why didn't you say he—?"

"He didn't hurt anyone, Avery, and Renee, there's danger here. I know you hear me, and it's all over the house, like a cloud. You have to leave. Please. Renee, please come with me. If you ever . . . if you ever trusted me, just do this one thing."

Renee and Louis? I stared at my grandmother, who had her eyes closed, her face pressed to the door, her fists still balled up against it.

"Stop it," she whispered. "I—I know what you are. I know what you can do. And Ben—"

"Ben and Avery are bound," Louis said. "And Avery hasn't run from it. Not until now. Something is going on, Renee, and I don't want to see you hurt. I still—" He broke off.

"I don't want to see you hurt," he said again. "And I don't want Avery hurt either."

"Ben is going to be arrested," Renee said. "He'll never hurt anyone again. Do you hear me, Louis? I *know* what he did."

"You think I'd harbor a killer? Renee, do you really—?" Louis's voice broke. I shivered because there was so much emotion in it and I hadn't—

I hadn't known Louis felt much of anything. But he did.

"Ben did not kill your son," Louis said. "He didn't kill anyone. Renee, I'm begging you, please—"

Renee put her hands over her ears and said, "Stop it. Just . . . stop it. Go and live in the woods and let me stumble through life as best I can and—" She paused, rested her head against the door. "If you ever cared for me, you'll leave."

"Renee—"

"Please. If you ever did care like you said, you'll go now. You'll go because it's the one thing I've ever asked of you since . . . since before."

Silence.

Nothing but silence, and I crept to the door, leaning against Renee, who was slumped over, crying silently. I looked through the peephole.

Louis was gone.

He was gone but Renee was still leaning against the door, her hands curling over her ears. She was still shaking.

"He left," I said, and touched her arm gently.

She moved her hands away and I told her again.

When I did, she closed her eyes—I saw them glistening wetly—but when she opened them they were dry.

"Good," she said. "We're safe here. And what he said about you and Ben, it isn't true at all. I know that. I mean, Ben hasn't been here long enough for you two to..." She trailed off, and I could tell she was thinking about the other night. About what she'd seen.

"Go back and get in the dining room like I said before," she said, her voice cracking. "Even if it's Ben, you stay put. Do you understand?"

"Grandma—"

"You know," she said, smiling at me, "I've gotten used to 'Renee.' When this is over, when we're safe, we'll have to talk about that. We'll talk about a lot of things. But now—" She pushed me toward the dining room. "Avery, you have to go. Hide. Do you understand me? *Hide.*"

I went and hid. I sat under the dining room table, sat covered by it, but it just seemed wrong.

I didn't want to hide. And besides, this was the first place I'd look if I was trying to find someone. If I was hunting them. And Ben was more than human; Ben would know exactly where to find me.

It would be so easy for him.

My heart kept seeing Ben looking at me. Kept remembering how he felt when he did. Kept hearing him swear he'd never hurt me.

I got out from under the table and sat on the floor by

the cabinet Renee kept her china in. Anyone who came into the room could see me.

And I would see them.

The doorbell rang. I tensed, then realized it was Ron. He'd come, just like he said he would, and now we were safe.

Everything was going to be okay now. Ben would—no. I had to stop thinking about him.

But my heart—my mind—cried out for him one last time before I got up and went to see Ron. To find out if Ben had been caught.

I could still feel him, even now. He was scared, so scared.

"Avery?" Ron called, and I pushed my feelings—pushed Ben—away and went out to see him. To hear what had happened to the Thantos family. To my parents. To me.

thirty-one

There you are," Ron said as I came out of the dining room, shifting a large bag on his shoulder. "I didn't know if you were still here. I thought you might have left because Ben had come by. I heard rumors you two were—"

"No," I said quickly. Maybe too quickly.

"Good," he said, not seeming to notice how fast I'd spoken. "Good for a lot of reasons, and I'm glad you stayed put. Has anything happened? Anyone come by the house? I came prepared, but still . . ."

I looked at Renee. She hadn't told Ron about Louis, then.

"No," I said. "We did what you said. We locked everything. All the windows. All the doors."

"Good," Ron said again. "Renee, my car isn't anywhere near here because I don't want to draw attention. Not until I know Ben has been caught, and I haven't radioed in that I'm here. I just don't want anyone knowing I'm here and risking—well, risking you two."

Renee blew out a breath, then nodded and said, "I wouldn't have thought of that. Sit down and we'll—well, I guess you'll tell us what happens now. Do you want a sandwich or anything?" Her voice was strained, but she sent a trembling smile toward me. A smile that said we were all right now. We were safe.

"No, don't go to any trouble," Ron said. "I want you to be comfortable. You and Avery both. You've been through enough. Too much. I'm so sorry for that."

"You didn't know," Renee said. "No one wants to think those stories could be real. They just—they are."

"John didn't believe them, but the forest still loved him plenty," Ron said and Renee nodded.

"You're right, he didn't believe them. Maybe if he had—"

"I know," Ron said. "But it hurts too much to go there, doesn't it? The forest really did love him, you know, almost like it was a person or something. We'd go hiking and he'd see things and I'd just get poison ivy and bug bites." He shook his head. "He wanted Woodlake to stay the same forever. He never saw what it could be."

He looked at me then. "He didn't want it to be like everyplace else. He'd say, 'No shopping malls, no roads that will take you to outlet malls and the interstate.'" He smiled. "Doesn't that sound just like him?"

"It does. He really loved the woods," I said. "I just . . . why would—?" I still couldn't bring myself to say "Ben." "Why did he and Mom die for that?"

Ron shook his head and said, "Renee, I think—there's a shadow over there, on the side of the house. You'd better close the curtains. Can you do that?"

"Sure," Renee said. She went over to the window, pulling the curtains closed. "Did you see something? Is it—?" She glanced at me. "Is it Ben?"

"I don't know," Ron said. "I sent everyone we had— even that FBI officer—out after him. It was probably just a rabbit. But it's better—it's better that no one see anything that happens now."

"Happens?" Renee said and I stared at Ron, standing there in his sheriff's uniform, a uniform I'd seen so many times, in town. Out at the house.

The house.

Night, that night, and Mom was frowning like she knew something was going on, like the tension around the house was too much, too thick, and she handed me the mushroom bag and told me to go, her voice urgent.

I went, sighing as I did, and wrinkled my nose at the smell of our compost heap as I went out the back door, as I headed into the forest and heard Ron step into the house. Heard him say, "John, we have to talk. You've got to be reasonable about this. I will make you listen, do you understand?"

"You," I said. "You were there. You came by right before my parents . . . before they died."

"Yes, I did," Ron said, and his voice was so pleasant. So calm, so nice—and then he opened the bag he was carrying.

"John and his damned forest, the one he loved with its plants and bugs and things," he said. "You know, no matter what I did, he just wouldn't sell his land to me. It's a shame, really."

It was then I saw the silver ax in his hand.

thirty-two

R on?" Renee said, her voice shocked, and he looked at her.

"You know Woodlake can be so much more than it is," he said. "And the woods have never been anything but torture to me my whole life. There's just a few pieces of land I need, and once I can talk good old Steve into getting them—and he will, because he wants this place to be a real town too. I know he offered you a very fair deal by the way, Renee. I was surprised you didn't agree. You hardly ever saw John. I saw him more than you did."

"You and Steve are working together?" Renee said, and Ron laughed.

"Steve? He's a way to make Woodlake better. He wants things, but he doesn't have the ability or stomach to follow through. Not like I do."

"But, Ron, you and John were friends," Renee said.

She took a step back, but there was nowhere to go. We'd locked all the windows. All the doors. And now the curtains were shut, and Ron's car was parked far away. No one could see in.

No one would know he was here.

No one would see him standing in front of us, a silver ax in one hand.

I bent over, gasping, not from fear, but from memory.

Finally—now, and too late—*I remembered.*

I'd gone to get mushrooms and I'd heard Dad's voice, I'd heard—

I'd heard him scream.

"You—" I said, staring at Ron, and I'd—

I'd run back toward the house after the screaming started but stopped short by a tree when I heard Mom say, "Avery isn't here. She's with a friend. And Ron, she's just a child."

"She's spent her whole life listening to you," Ron had said, and raised his ax. "She won't see that if these woods are gone, Woodlake will thrive. It can finally become a real town. Now, where is she? I know she doesn't know many people at the high school. It's my job to know these things, you know. Just— Debby, you can even sign the papers, all right? Just sign them and I'll be on my way and everything will be fine. You'll like living in town. I'll pull some strings, have Steve get you a nice place. I can pull all kinds of strings for you."

"You won't let me live," Mom whispered, and Ron sighed, then said, "I did always tell John you were too smart for your

own good," and then silver—the silver ax—flew through the air, Ron—

Ron breaking my mother with it. Swinging that silver ax over and over, blood and silver flying. Shining.

And as he did it, he was humming.

Ron was humming and moving so fast it was like he wasn't human, like my parents weren't human, like they were just pieces of meat he had to cut apart, and I pushed a hand against my mouth so I wouldn't scream, and I tried to close my eyes, but I couldn't—

I looked and saw the silver gleaming, moving again and again and again.

I saw Ron kill my parents and then walk back the way he came, the ax—bright red now—dripping as he did. I saw him stop, wipe it against the ground.

He was still humming. They were dead, gone by his hand. And yet he kept right on humming.

"You killed them," I said. "You killed my parents. And all because you wanted their land? You chopped them up like meat and you *hummed* while you did it."

"And here I thought you didn't remember. I was so angry about Deputy Sharpe finding you before I could—at least until you looked at me with your big blank eyes," Ron said almost cheerfully, and swung the ax in a slow, lazy circle. Renee grabbed my arm and pulled me to the back of the room, steering us toward the kitchen.

"I guess if I'd just shown you this"—he gestured at the ax—"you might have remembered, and, well, if Sharpe hadn't found you, things would be very different. Frankly, Avery, I still don't know how you survived that tree falling. I thought for sure that would do it. But you just keep on living, don't you?"

He smiled, all shining, hungry teeth. "I have to say, I'm surprised you think Ben Dusic killed your parents. I mean, the new boy in town? Really? That's just—well, I couldn't have picked better myself."

He looked at Renee then, still smiling. "And you, talking about the woods and stories?" He shook his head. "Babbling, frankly. What was it you said? Oh yes, 'the stories are true.' If I'd known you were going senile, I'd just have signed the papers for you, passed them along to Steve, and then claimed you'd done it, with me, the sheriff, as witness, and then all this could have been avoided. It's a shame, really."

"I'll sign," Renee said. "Whatever papers you want or need, I'll sign them. You can have the woods and do whatever you want and we'll just—"

"What?" Ron said. "Forget this happened? No, Renee, I don't think so. And even if I believed you—which I don't—there's still Avery. She saw me, you know. I had to suffer the bad luck of someone else finding her first and I thought she'd remember but she didn't, and then—well, I wasn't going to leave her alone, but I was going to give her some time. Let her try to have a normal life before she killed herself."

He looked at me. "I was going to make it easy for you,

Avery. Just a simple hanging. It would have been painless. Not now, though. I'm sorry about that."

"No, you're not," I said, and thought of the evil Ben had shown me that lay in wait around my parents' home. That had been Ron.

Ron.

He'd cut the tree. He was the wrongness that Ben—and I—had felt that day in the forest. "You're not sorry for anything. You killed my parents and the Thantos family too. And all for land? You're a million times worse than Steve because you want the woods to go away, don't you? But the forest isn't yours, Ron. It won't ever be yours, no matter how much of it you chop away."

"Quit it," he said, almost growling at me. "I have what I want now. You and Renee die and John's land is mine, free and clear with no messy waiting period. Then the forest—oh, it will shrink. It will shrivel. It'll all be over."

He looked at me. "It's been so much work. No one really appreciates a woodsman's craft, you know? Knowing what needs to be taken down. How to set things up so it all falls into place without your hard work ever being seen or appreciated."

"I told someone," I said, making myself look right at him. "I told Ben everything and we decided this was the only way to get you to confess to what you'd done. Everything you say is being heard right now. It's being taped too."

"Really?" Ron said. "Well, that's—" He laughed.

"Avery, you just aren't a good liar. No, you actually believed that the new boy in town killed your parents, and like I said, I couldn't have asked for anything better. I'll go to the school on Monday, lift his prints, and they'll end up here. I'll solve the murders, the town will be crime-free, and people will sleep easy again."

He looked at Renee. "Put that platter down," he said, his voice gentle. "Your holiday serving dish isn't going to stop me. It'll just upset me. And Avery can tell you, I don't do all that well when I'm upset. Do I, Avery?"

I could see everything now, remember everything.

I'd crawled out from behind the tree after Ron had gone. I'd crawled to my parents and tried to save them, tried to put them back together again, but I couldn't, and after that I didn't move because I didn't want to leave them. I didn't want them to be dead and no one would believe me, no one would believe the sheriff could do anything like what he had, but I had to tell someone and I would. I just needed to sit for a minute. I just needed to not think about what I'd heard and seen, needed to not think about how Ron had raised that ax over and over and over again like it was nothing. Like my parents were nothing.

"No, you don't like being upset," I whispered, and my back hit the living room wall. Renee and I had gone as far as we could, and I felt her reaching back behind me, could tell she was straining for something.

"Ah, the living room," Ron said. "Does this make what's going to happen now ironic?"

"Don't ask me about irony, you little—" Renee said, and stepped in front of me, both hands holding the piece of wood we'd been sanding, the one that had been on the kitchen table. The one she'd clearly been able to reach.

The wood hit Ron right in the face, and it hit him hard, landing with a loud pop that made him stagger back, then fall. I stared at Renee.

"He always did like to talk," she said. "Stay back because I'm going to make sure he isn't going to get up for a while."

And then Ron stood up, blood pouring from his face, his mouth twisted, and he started to run toward us, the ax swinging.

"Run!" Renee yelled, and we both did, scrambled into the kitchen and moved out of the way as the ax slammed into the kitchen table, splitting it in two.

"Now you've made me angry," Ron said, his face blood red. He lifted the ax again.

"No," I yelled, and grabbed a kitchen chair. I swung it out toward him and felt the ax hit it, felt the blow shatter the wood, the shock of it vibrating up my arms.

"Enough of this," Ron said, and grabbed me, pulling me toward him with one hand as the ax lifted again.

I watched it start to fall.

And then there was glass everywhere, the sliding door at the back of the kitchen—the one that looked out onto

the porch Renee and I were slowly starting to build—
shattering, and I was on the floor, staring as Ron swung
the ax down.

Staring at Ben as he looked at me, as he yelled, "Run!"
As the ax hit him.

thirty-three

N o," I screamed, and Renee grabbed my hand and yanked me toward her, yanked me outside and pressed something into my hand, said, "Avery, go back in and hit that bastard as hard as you can."

I looked at her, and she said, "You heard me." Then she ran back into the house, ran right back toward Ron.

She hit him with one of our post-hole diggers, the metal end of it turned toward him, and it caught him right across the neck. He staggered back, endless, empty fury in his eyes.

I saw Ben on the floor, so still—too still—and I ran as hard and fast as I could back into the house.

I froze as Ron saw me, but when he tried to raise his ax again, I was able to move because I knew I had to. I lifted the post-hole digger Renee had pressed into my hand, so scared it was like it weighed nothing, and then I slammed it down on his arm.

Ron screamed, and the ax fell free, landed on the floor.

"My arm!" he yelled. "You bitches, you broke my arm!"

And then Ben stood up.

There was blood on him, running down the right side of his body, streaming from his shoulder, but he didn't seem to notice it.

"A glancing blow," he said, staring at Ron. His eyes were silver, nothing but silver, and his whole body rippled, starting to shift, to change.

He said, "No one hurts Avery," the words coming out slurred, changing into something different. Into a cry.

An animal's cry.

"Don't," Renee said, her voice sharp. "Don't you change now. Avery, tell him to listen to you, to come back. Tell him!"

"Ben," I said, and he froze, his body twisted, starting to change. He looked at me and what I saw—

What I saw wasn't human.

But it was Ben, and I needed him.

Ben shuddered. I felt what he wanted—he ached to hurt Ron. He desperately craved his own brand of justice for what Ron had done.

"I was so scared," he whispered. "So angry, so hurt, but I couldn't stay away. I had to come and make sure you were okay, and then, when I realized Ron was trying to kill you . . ."

I swallowed.

What he'd seen had made him do something no human could do.

What he'd seen had saved us.

"Thank you," I said, and Ben shivered again.

Now he was himself, the Ben I knew, shaking and bleeding all over Renee's kitchen.

"Avery," he said, and I went to him. I touched his face, his beautiful, perfect face.

"I'm sorry," I said. "I'm so sorry. I trusted you, I did, but I got scared. It won't happen again. I swear it won't."

"I—thank you," Ben whispered, and then he collapsed. He hit the floor hard, his silver eyes closing.

I screamed, but Renee grabbed my arms and said, "Avery, you called him back from changing, and that hurts. It's not the ax. That's just a flesh wound. Ben just . . . he has to rest. We're all right now. We *are*."

She made her way over to the phone and I watched her dial 911. I sank down next to Ben and took his hands in mine. I willed him to open his eyes and look at me. To see me.

Around us I heard noises, faint at first but then growing louder, and then people were trying to separate us; people were trying to ask me things, their words coming so fast I couldn't understand.

"All right," Renee said very loudly, and quiet fell, everyone turning to look at her. "Ron Jericho just tried to kill me and my granddaughter and admitted to killing

my son, my daughter-in-law, and three other people. You take him and that ax of his and you get it all out of here. You do that, and then you ask your questions, bring in your whatever. Is that clear?"

"I—" someone said, and Renee said, "Is that clear?" again, her voice ringing out, and that was when I knew for sure who Renee used to be.

Once, she'd been like me. She'd had what I had with the woods, and possibly had with Louis what me and Ben had too. But she'd turned away from all of it.

I looked down at Ben. He groaned, softly, and opened his eyes.

"Are you all right?" he whispered.

My grandmother had turned away from what could have been. I wasn't going to.

"Yes," I said. "Just stay here with me, all right?"

"Always," Ben said, and around us people kept moving, kept talking, but I didn't see or hear them. Not really.

All I saw was Ben, and I knew that all he saw was me. The whole world didn't—it was there, but it didn't matter.

Or at least it didn't until Ben had to go to the hospital.

thirty-four

I wasn't allowed to ride with him in the ambulance but Renee took me in her car, and we followed it to the hospital.

"Don't worry," she said to me as we turned into the hospital parking lot. She touched my hair, fingers resting on the blood red strand that still lay there. "People like Ben can be very persuasive when they want to be. He'll be fine. There won't be any trouble with the hospital at all."

Renee and I were definitely going to have to talk about what she knew about the woods, and we were also going to have to talk about her and Louis. We were going to have to talk about a lot of things.

But not now. Now I needed to find Ben, and when I did, he wasn't in the emergency room like I'd thought he'd be. He was just sitting in the waiting room, sitting there like nothing was wrong with him at all.

"You—" I said, rushing to him. "I saw the ax hit you, and even if it wasn't that deep, you'll probably still need stitches."

He shook his head. "I heal really fast, and I definitely don't need to see a doctor. My blood work wouldn't be normal, and the questions it would raise—I can't afford that."

He looked at Renee, who'd come into the waiting room as well.

She looked right back at him, silent for a moment, and then she said, "You sure you'll be all right?"

"Yes."

"Good. Still, have Louis look at your shoulder."

Ben nodded.

"And tell Louis—" Renee broke off. "Never mind that." She smiled. "Later, we'll talk about how you're going to pay me back for the door." Ben smiled back and she said, "Avery, I'm going to go talk to the police now. You don't mind staying here, do you?"

"No," I said. Renee smiled again, leaned over, and kissed the top of my head.

"You did good," she whispered, and then she walked away.

I looked at Ben. He was pale, and there was dried blood all over him. He was everything, and I wanted to hold him and never ever let him go.

There was a loud noise by the door, and then a cluster of people pushed their way inside.

"I'm telling you, I saw something," Ron screamed. "I saw something that wasn't human, and it's real, the stories about this town and its woods are real. The wolves are here and they're coming! They are all coming! I see them right now!"

"Nice try," a dark-haired man leaning over Ron said. "But at the FBI, we don't take kindly to being called out to help with cases where it turns out the town sheriff is a mass murderer who also happens to be hiding hundreds of thousands of dollars from real estate deals. You won't be going to any psych ward, no matter how many stories you tell." He turned to someone and said, "Make sure Steve Browning knows that if he wants any sort of deal, he'll start talking about everything Ron Jericho asked him to do."

"The woods!" Ron screamed. "They'll live in the woods and I was right to want them gone! I was right and there will be blood, so much blood. No one will be safe. No one!" He thrashed and looked right at me. "Not even *you*."

I shivered. Ben looked at me, but I felt more than his gaze, more than Ron's words. I felt the forest.

I felt the forest, and it knew something was coming too.

"Keep trying those stories, Mr. Jericho," the man said, and Ron was wheeled away, everyone staring after him.

Everyone except me and Ben.

We were looking at each other.

"You sensed something then, didn't you?" he said.

"The forest is—I don't know. Something is coming."

"We'll be ready," he said, and took my hands in his.

"Your hair hasn't changed," he said, and like Renee had, he reached out and touched the strand that had been marked.

"I cut it off before," I said. "I thought it meant death, but I think it means something else. I think it's the forest mourning. It feels things too, and I'm going to leave my hair alone. Let it remind me of what happened. Who we've lost."

I looked at him, twining my fingers tightly with his. "That, and who's still here. Who I need in my life."

I took a deep breath, finally ready to say what was in my heart and had been all along.

"I love you," I said, and Ben sucked in a breath, whispered, "Avery," and then he kissed me.

Right there, in the emergency room waiting area, he kissed me and it was enough, it was more than enough.

I had lost so much, and so had he, but we'd found something too.

We'd found each other. We'd found love, and that was something we both would do anything to hold on to.

It was something we both wanted to keep safe no matter what.

We *would* keep it safe, and I sensed his certainty and mine twine together, our hearts and minds beating as one.

I felt the forest feel it too and sigh, let go of a little of the worry it carried.

"So, maybe you and I could try doing something normal," Ben said.

I smiled at him. "I'd like that. Maybe we could go to the movies this weekend?"

"Or you could tell me why a town called Woodlake has no lake?"

"What can I say?" I told him. "The people that first moved here were hopeful. And you know how it is with hope, right?"

"I do now," he said, and then he kissed me again, his smiling mouth matching my own.

Acknowledgments

Thanks to Margaret Miller for believing in me and this book—and then going the extra mile. Plus several more!

Thanks also go to Jessica Brearton and Diana Fox, who believed in this book from the beginning.